THE WAY OF WATER

By

Caridad Svich

NoPassport Press
& Welsh Fargo Stage Company Edition

The Way of Water
Copyright 2013, 2012 by Caridad Svich.

1st Preview Edition for Welsh Fargo Stage, 2013
2nd Edition copyright 2016.

For performance enquiries of this script please
contact csvich21@caridadsvich.com
Or newdramatists@newdramatists.org

NoPassport Press
www.nopassport.org

ISBN: 978-1-365-27378-0

*NoPassport is an unincorporated theatre alliance and press
dedicated to the production, advocacy and publication of
works for live performance expressive of aesthetic and
cultural diversity. NoPassport is a sponsored project of
Fractured Atlas in New York City.*

Welsh Fargo Stage Company

ON THE EDGE: The Ian Rowlands Season

The Welsh, award winning, internationally, highly regarded playwright Ian Rowlands was once described by one of Wales major critics as "undisputedly one of Wales most interesting and exciting playwrights". He and the Welsh Fargo Stage Company's Artistic Director, Michael Kelligan first met, as young actors over twenty years ago and have since remained very good friends and as writer and director they have developed an excellent professional, working relationship.

Rowlands is an International Associate of The Lark Play Development Center in New York. He was there in 2012 for a reading of his play *Desire Lines*. Whilst there he heard a reading of Caridad Svich's play *The Way of Water*. He sent a copy of the play to Kelligan, thinking it would make an ideal play to be read in Kelligan's company's On The Edge project.

The On The Edge project, funded by the Arts Council of Wales, now in its ninth year, presents script-held performances of plays mainly by Welsh playwrights and other Wales based writers. From time to time he has imported plays from the rest of the UK and abroad in order that Welsh writers and audiences are able to widen their knowledge and understanding of contemporary play writing on a wider basis. His first production of a play from the USA was Neil LaBute's *The Mercy Seat*.

Kelligan was very impressed by the beauty of the writing of *The Way of Water* and knowing that very few people in the UK would have any knowledge the awful problems that the Gulf of Mexico Bay oil disaster was causing people living along the Louisiana coast was an additional drive to see the play presented in March at his base at The Chapter Arts Centre in Cardiff and at the company's other two touring venues in Wales, The Dylan Thomas Centre in Swansea and the newly built Riverfront Theatre in Newport. All three are thriving coastal cities.

Kelligan has constructed his spring 2013 On The Edge season around his connection with Ian Rowlands. The first play presented, *A Nice Drink* by new writer Jude Garner won the Drama Association of Wales One Act play competition, the judge was Rowlands. It was developed into a full-length play by the Welsh Fargo Stage Company and presented in February.

Rowlands was planning a new work *Fragments of Journeys Towards the Horizon*. The play is the beginning of a longer-term collaboration between Rowlands and the Dutch writer / director, Jeroen van den Berg (also an International Lark Associate,). It is a through the looking glass reflection upon friendship, cancer and the nature of collaboration itself. Van den Berg is currently producing a parallel Dutch text. Both texts will be re-worked and merged to form a meta-text that will form the basis of a presentation at the Oerol Festival, NL in June. Rowland section of the script will be presented On The Edge in April

The final play in the On The Edge season is a revival of a play from a company Rowlands founded some years ago, *Sex and Power at The Beau Rivage* by Welsh writer and publisher Lewis Davies. The play concerns DH Lawrence and his wife Frieda entertaining the young Welsh short story writer just on the brink of fame, Rhys Davies. This production will complete the season.

The Way of Water
by Caridad Svich

Cast
Jimmy Robichaux...........Nick Wayland-Evans
Yuki Gonzalo Skow........Dick Bradnum
Rosalie Robichaux.........Polly Kilpatrick
Neva Skow.................Rebecca Knowles

Directed by Bethan Morgan

The play was read at The Lark Centre, New York
along with Ian Rowlands' play *Desire Lines* in 2012.
It is produced by Welsh Fargo Stage Company March
2013.

The Lark Play Development Centre is a laboratory for
new voices and new ideas, providing playwrights
and their collaborators with resources to develop
their work in a supportive yet rigorous environment
and encouraging artists to define their own goals and
creative processes in pursuit of a unique vision. We
embrace new and diverse perspectives here at home
and in all corners of the world,

Caridad Svich (Playwright) received a 2012 OBIE Award for Lifetime Achievement in the theatre, and the 2011 American Theatre Critics Association Primus Prize for her play *The House of the Spirits*, based on the novel by Isabel Allende. She has been short-listed for the PEN Award in Drama four times, including in the year 2012 for her play *Magnificent Waste*. In the 2012-13 season: 2012 Edgerton Foundation New Play Award round two recipient GUAPA received a rolling world premiere courtesy of NNPN at Borderlands Theater in Arizona, Miracle Theatre in Oregon and Phoenix Theater in Indiana. Her play *Spark* received multiple readings across the US, including a reading at the Cherry Lane Theatre produced by TEL and Mannatee Films under Scott Schwartz' direction, and a special reading at Cummins Theatre in Western Australia in November 2012 to honor war veterans. Among her key work are *12 Ophelias, Iphigenia Crash Land Falls…, Fugitive Pieces, Any Place But Here, Alchemy of Desire/Dead-Man's Blues..* Her works are published by Intellect UK, Eyecorner Press, Seagull Books, TCG, Smith & Kraus, Manchester University Press, Playscripts, Broadway Play Publishing and more.

Bethan Morgan (Director) has worked in TV, film, stage and radio for over 20 years. She has worked as an actor/musician in the West End and for many companies across the country, such as Bolton Octagon, Coventry Belgrade and Cardiff's Sherman

Theatre. She is also an accomplished singer/songwriter, Musical Director and Director. She has acted in 6 productions for the On The Edge seasons, composed original music for 2 and this will be the 4th piece she has directed. Bethan is also Co-director of Mercury Theatre Wales and is looking forward to directing their production of SPANGLED next month.

Rebecca Knowles (Neva), born in Edinburgh, graduated from the University of Glamorgan and the Royal Welsh College of Music and Drama with a degree in Theatre and Media Drama. Based in Cardiff since 2001 she has toured extensively with numerous theatre companies and has performed at the Traverse Theatre, Edinburgh and Leicester Haymarket as well as many screen appearances. Previous roles include 'The Snow Queen', Lady Macbeth and Viola in Twelfth Night. Rebecca was most recently seen in Who Killed the Elephant directed by Mathilde Lopez and performed at Chapter Arts Centre. This is her 5th outing with the Welsh Fargo Theatre Company.

Polly Kilpatrick (Rosalie) trained at The Royal Welsh College of Music & Drama, graduating in 1990 with 'The Principal's Prize for Drama.' Her career in Wales began with Wales Actors Company, touring castles, playing Lady Macduff in 'Macbeth,' Hero in 'Much Ado About Nothing,' Portia in 'Julius Caesar' and Ophelia in 'Hamlet.' Polly has also toured extensively with Oxfordshire Touring Theatre, Snap Theatre,

English Shakespeare Company and a European tour playing Hobby in John Godber's 'Teechers.' Polly has also appeared in 'Emmerdale' for ITV playing Jennifer Dobbs.

Dick Bradnum (Yuki) read English at the University of Birmingham and then went on to train at the Royal Welsh College of Music and Drama and the Institute of Education, UCL. He was a founder member of the Custard Factory Theatre Company. Acting credits include Romeo and Juliet and Macbeth (English Shakespeare Company), The Office, My Hero and High Hopes (BBCTV). He has appeared in many Radio Dramas, and was for several years a regular MC on the comedy circuit. His recent performance as Malvolio in Twelfth Night at York Theatre Royal was described as "a masterclass". Dick also works with young people, teaching and lecturing; and writes and delivers interactive training programmes for corporate clients.

Nick Wayland-Evans (Jimmy) is now best known as part of the Classical Brits award-winning choir but up until winning the TV talent show Last Choir Standing three years ago his main focus was acting. The success of Only Men Aloud has taken him away from acting apart from the occasional role-play and teaching work. Originally from Builth Wells, Nick moved to Cardiff in 2001 and now lives in Maesteg. One of nine siblings he has enjoyed a long relationship with youth theatre including working at Sherman Cymru .He explains, "I came across acting initially as a musician when I joined the Mid Powys Youth Theatre as a founder member in 1986. Under the direction of Greg Cullen and Guy Roderick, I was soon drawn into the world of acting and haven't looked back since! Over the years I have worked with companies including Gwent Theatre, Theatr Na n'og and Hijinx. I have been fortunate in working with a wide range of performers, writers, directors, designers, practitioners and designers, all of whom I regard as very dear friends and all of whom have influenced me immensely."

Script History:

This play was developed in a 2011 Winter Writers Retreat, 2012 Roundtable Reading, and 2012 Studio Retreat directed by Daniella Topol, all at the Lark Play Development Center, New York City.

A NoPassport theatre alliance international reading scheme for the play at 50 venues across the US and abroad, including venues in South Africa, Australia, Germany, Brazil, England, New York, Los Angeles, Chicago and more, from April to early June 2012. Dramaturges: Heather Helinsky and R. Alex Davis. For more information, documentation and blog series visit www.nopassport.org/wayofwater

A version of the play launched the first issue of the electronic publication StageReads edited by Meredith Lynsey Schade and Jody Christopherson in September 2012.

It received a workshop production at Frank Theatre in Minneapolis, Minnesota in 2012 directed by Wendy Knox.

It was produced as a touring version in Wales by Welsh Fargo Stage Company in 2013 as part of their Ian Rowlands season.

Introduction to THE WAY OF WATER
By Henry Godinez, Resident Artistic Associate,
Goodman Theatre, Chicago

*[This introduction is published in the subscription-based,
industry-aimed new play e-book platform StageReads LLC
founded by Meredith Lynsey Schade and Jody
Christopherson. StageReads launched with the publication
of Caridad Svich's* The Way of Water. *This introduction
is reprinted with Henry Godinez's permission.]*

In the United States, in this age of 24 hour news
networks, the shelf life of even a major disaster is
somewhere between that of fresh fish and a gallon of
milk. Unless of course that fish comes from the Gulf
of Mexico, in which case it could last much longer,
like say, a good sex scandal. Without the luxury of
being able to count on the scrupulous nature of
mainstream American journalism alone to keep
pivotal events alive in our collective memory, the
only sure way to chronicle our mistakes of the past in
order to prevent their return in the future is to
enshrine them in art. Fortunately such is the case
with the BP oil disaster in the Gulf of Mexico in 2010,
which is now lovingly and movingly enshrined
Caridad Svich's searing new play *The Way of Water*.
　　The BP oil spill remains the worst marine
drilling disaster in our nation's history, gushing
nearly five million gallons of crude oil into the Gulf of
Mexico and devastating thousands of miles of fragile
wetlands, beaches and commercial fishing areas.

After two years, too many questions remain unanswered, though it is evident that negligence due to cost cutting efforts on the part of BP was certainly at the heart of the accident, which also incidentally, killed eleven men when their Deepwater Horizon platform exploded. Two years later scientists are beginning to see the lasting effects of the spill in an alarming number of mutated fish, crabs and shrimp, while dolphin and whales continue to be found dead at almost double the normal rate.

Within that all too brief network news worthy shelf life of the BP oil disaster, there was time to speculate about the economic ramifications; the cost of lost revenue to the fishing and vacation industries, property values, and even the cost of gas at the pump. There was the occasional tugging at the heart strings story about the after effects of the spill on the coastal areas and the wildlife, the now all too common televised scenes of volunteers scrubbing water fowl covered in thick crude oil. But rarely is a disaster like the BP oil spill sexy enough to have a shelf life that allows for the consideration of its long term effects on human beings. Then again it could simply be that my more cynical self contemplates the possibility that some nefarious and hugely powerful unseen group of select individuals simply maneuver it that way, after all, that would be bad for business. The disaster may have vanished from the headlines and the airwaves but the after effects are ominously still in the water and slowly rising to the surface.

Skepticism and paranoia aside, it nonetheless remains the task of the artist to, as Hamlet says, "hold as 'twere the mirror up to nature; to show virtue her own feature, scorn her own image, and the very age and body of the time, his form and pressure." In *The Way of Water*, Caridad Svich holds a powerful human mirror up to reflect the less glamorous edges of society. Not one that reflects the images of wealthy landowners along the coast whose stretches of pristine sand beaches and multimillion dollar vacation homes have been degraded by tar balls, but the average working class people whose livelihoods and very lives are compromised by their dependence on water contaminated by dispersants which linger long after the crude oil is no longer visible. It is a play about four friends who are as much a part of their particular environment and the nature that has sustained it, as those wildfowl that wash up encased in crude oil.

The play delicately evokes the image of common man Jimmy Robichaux, a fishing man from way back, and his struggle to simply carve out an honorable living around the waters that have nurtured his family for generations. He is a beautifully drawn, profoundly human character, wrestling with old ways and new demons. Jimmy's personal struggles are manifested so honestly within the larger context of the BP oil spill that the play never feels like an indictment, at least not in the moment. This is a play about a group of friends just trying to get by in a world whose promises and dreams have all passed them by. It is also a play about taking action, about realizing that sometimes just speaking out can make a difference. But the play's great strength lies in its humanity.

Having grown up in the south, in Texas, Alabama and Louisiana, I know the ring of authenticity in a true southerner when I hear it. I know the sounds, the idiosyncratic choice of words, the tempos. More importantly, I know the sound of humility and honor in a southern voice and in all these case, Caridad has clearly done her homework and created characters that ring true. Certainly honor is not an exclusively southern trait but in my experience, in the south it is a trait that is not exclusive to class or wealth either. This inherent, passionate, stubborn adherence to honor is one of the most compelling and integral motivating factors in *The Way of Water*. It is the rope at the center of the characters' personal tug-a-wars, it is at the center of the conflict of the play, the very thing in each of the characters, but especially in Jimmy, that drives them to act. It is an essence that Caridad has made painfully real.

Many a great play has been written about corporate negligence and devastating catastrophes but what makes *The Way of Water* so compelling is the way it exposes the after effects of such sensational events in the most real of human terms. Given the way our society seems content to turn a blind eye to the huge power of corporate financial influence, as made evident for instance in the Citizens United ruling by the U.S. Supreme Court, it must remain the task of the artist to sound the alarm bell when long term profits take precedence over the seemingly short life of a man. Yet at its best, theatre must be more than a political or social protest. For Hamlet's intention I'm sure was not just to show "the age and body of the time, his form and pressure", but to actually instigate change. *The Way of Water* does that very effectively as all good art does, by representing humanity so truthfully and universally that we cannot help but see ourselves at the center of the story.

THE WAY OF WATER by Caridad Svich

Full-length. Two acts. Cast: 2 men (30s), 2 women (30s). Set: single, two-location set. Running time: 2 hours.

Synopsis: _The Way of Water_ is a play that pits the aftermath of the Deepwater Horizon 2010 BP oil spill in the Gulf of Mexico next to the lives of those affected by it. It's a story about four people making do as best they can, living their lives, and trying to stay afloat in the land of many compromised dreams, as the devastation of a health and environmental crisis scandal in the US Gulf is played out on a human scale. It's a play about poverty in America, rumors and truth, what is said and what gets written, and the quest for an honorable life.

Characters:
JIMMY ROBICHAUX, fisherman, 30s, impulsive, passionate, quick-tempered, proud
YUKI GONZALO SKOW, his friend and fellow fisherman, 30s, of mixed race [pronunciation of surname rhymes with "snow"]
ROSALIE ROBICHAUX, Jimmy's wife, 30s, strong yet vulnerable, sensual, practical, a bit of a dreamer
NEVA SKOW, Yuki's wife, 30s, steady, strong, dryly funny, supportive, and a bit guarded [pronounced Nee-vah]

Time & Place: The present, preferably many months after April 20, 2010, in a small town in coastal, southeastern Louisiana in Plaquemines Parish, along the Gulf of Mexico.

Background: An explosion on April 20, 2010, aboard the Deepwater Horizon, a drilling rig working on a well for the oil company BP one mile below the surface of the Gulf of Mexico, led to the largest "accidental" oil spill disaster in history. Residents who live along the coast of the Gulf of Mexico, all the way from Terrebonne Parish, Louisiana, to well into western Florida, continue to suffer acute symptoms attributed to ongoing exposure to toxic chemicals being released from BP's crude oil and the toxic Corexit dispersants used to sink it. Thousands of deaths along the Gulf Coast region have been linked to this toxic damage. This devastation is being deemed by many in the health and science field as the equivalent of Agent Orange in Vietnam.

PART ONE: Scene One

Exterior. Day. By the water. Bright sun peeks through the clouds of an early morning. Yuki and Jimmy are fishing.

JIMMY: Gone the way of water.
YUKI: You think?
JIMMY: Ain't bitin' for nothin'.
YUKI: Gotta wait.
JIMMY: Been waitin'.
YUKI: There's time.
JIMMY: If I ain't catch me a bucket, I ain't got nothin' for the day. What's Rosalie gonna say? Huh? She gonna haul my ass.
YUKI: She's a good woman.
JIMMY: You live with her?
YUKI: Nice lady.
JIMMY: Yeah. But she got helluva temper. Helluva and a day. Make no mistake.
YUKI: Makes pretty flowers.
JIMMY: Craft store maven. What are we gonna do with all them fake flowers?
YUKI: Sell them.
JIMMY: Huh.
YUKI: People like pretty things.
JIMMY: People got two dollars in their wallet, they ain't gonna spend them on flowers. They go to MickeyD's or Dunkin Donuts n' get a two dollar breakfast that will last them all day. Fill their stomach; that's what people wanna do.
YUKI: Sausage and hotcakes.

JIMMY: McGriddles and a biscuit.

YUKI: Shoulda had me breakfast this mornin.'

JIMMY: Didn't have?

YUKI: Forgot.

JIMMY: Christ, Yuki.

YUKI: I know.

JIMMY: Can't fish on an empty stomach. How many times I gotta tell you?

YUKI: I forgot.

JIMMY: Don't know what I'm gonna do with you.

YUKI: I'll remember next time.

JIMMY: You'll remember 'cuz I'll drag you into a MickeyD's, that's what.

Fish on the line.

YUKI: Somethin'?

JIMMY: Tuggin'.

YUKI: … Nasty yellowfish. Let it go.

JIMMY: I will.

YUKI: Nasty fish's no good.

JIMMY: Rotten stinker kill my business.

Fish tosses fish to the side, in the boat. A moment.

YUKI: All along here…

JIMMY: Yeh.

YUKI: Whole stretch…

JIMMY: Pretty soon, we'll have nothin' left. … Don't know how those oil pigs do it. First in Valdez way back when… My daddy said "This time for sure somebody's gonna take them to task." … Big news for a while, then it faded away; like everythin' else.

YUKI: The way it all goes.

JIMMY: Goes as it goes as it goes. Memories like sieves in this country.

YUKI: It's human nature, Jimmy. Like, when Neva and I started hookin' up… it was, like, we forgot about everybody else we'd dated before and focused on each other.

JIMMY: Talkin' history, Yuki, not love.

YUKI: Love and history is the same thing. People like to forget. Move on. Way of nature, way of water.

JIMMY: N water gets foul and who gets fucked?

YUKI: We clean it up, don't we?

JIMMY: Well…

YUKI: They hire us out, we put our noses right in the thick of the dirty oil. They own us all.

JIMMY: Don't own me.

YUKI: …

JIMMY: Don't look at me like that.

YUKI: Ain't lookin' [at] nothin'.

JIMMY: Lookin' like you wanna look. I ain't your lady Neva you can stare me down just like that.

YUKI: Ain't starin'.

JIMMY: See your eyes.

YUKI: Lookin' clear way somewhere else.

JIMMY: Like you wanna put the fear of God in me.

YUKI (*to self*): Jesus…

JIMMY (*cont*): Ain't nobody put the fear of God in me. Nobody but God Himself.

YUKI: Let it go, Jimmy.
JIMMY: Y' hear what I'm sayin'?
YUKI: Let it go. All right?!

A moment. Jimmy is disoriented.

YUKI: What?
JIMMY: All goin' round for a second.
YUKI: Dizzy again? Gotta see doctor 'bout that. Can't go round havin' fits and things.
JIMMY: You ever seen me havin' a fit? I'm fine, Yuki.
YUKI: Dizzy.
JIMMY: Fine.

A moment.

YUKI: …Air's burnin'.
JIMMY: Everythin's burnin'.

A moment.

JIMMY: My cousin in Waxahachie got himself all burned up.
YUKI: Huh?
JIMMY: Remember that chemical fire on the news?
YUKI: No.
JIMMY: Chemical plant that had an explosion. Sent thick plumes of smoke up into the sky for hours.
YUKI: When was this?
JIMMY: Some time back.
YUKI: Round here?

JIMMY: Waxahachie, bro. Texas.

YUKI: Oh. And this was on the news?

JIMMY: Flames devoured buildings. You didn't see it?

YUKI: No.

JIMMY: What news you watch?

YUKI: What's on.

JIMMY: Nasty fire. My cousin Ray worked in that plant. Makin' some kind of ammonia they use in products and things… Got burned bad. Company says there was no one in the plant when the explosion happened.

YUKI: He got hush money, then?

JIMMY: Hush peanuts.

YUKI: Somethin', though.

JIMMY: Nickels and dimes. What cousin Ray gonna do with nickels and dimes when he got hospital bill eating his ass?

YUKI: Sue 'em.

JIMMY: Ray says he'll just stay quiet. Don't want scandal. Used to be a real fighter, y'know? Now, he gonna sign some paper says he wadn't even in the plant.

YUKI: Talk to him.

JIMMY: … Sometimes I think what Ray's goin' through, what we're goin' through…is just gonna go away in some mad toxic smoke dream cooked up by some smooth little badass sittin' in some chair in some glass dome somewhere lookin' out over the bought-out ocean. End of line, I am. Goddamn end of line.

YUKI: Don't say that.

JIMMY: Got nothin' else.

YUKI: Fish come 'round, Jimmy.

JIMMY: Come 'round and squat.

YUKI: We'll make somethin'.

JIMMY: Ain't made in a long time. What we gonna live on? I mean, you got…

YUKI: What you talkin'?

JIMMY: Your lady Neva's workin'.

YUKI: So's Rosalie.

JIMMY: Piddley-ass part time.

YUKI: It's somethin'.

JIMMY: Man, you got it made.

YUKI: How I got it made?

JIMMY: Bank.

YUKI: Bank? Shit. We're the same, bro.

JIMMY: Same boat?

YUKI: How many times you been to my house? You see anything there worth somethin'? Neva works. Yeh. But we got baby comin'. And I got a pile of bills I don't know what… Wake up every day thinkin' how I'm gonna figure things out.

JIMMY *(light joke)*: Lottery.

YUKI: You shittin' me now?

JIMMY: You got your house, man. Not everybody's got a paid off house.

YUKI: Worth shit.

JIMMY: Worth somethin'.

YUKI: …Listen, we'll do all right. As long as we get some fish…

JIMMY: Mad shit waste. … And I ain't even had me turkey bacon and eggs over easy yet.

YUKI: Thought you said-

JIMMY: Had me coffee, walked out the door.

YUKI: Shit.

JIMMY: Uh-huh.

YUKI: That's messed up.

JIMMY: Coulda had me turkey bacon and eggs over easy.

YUKI: Sunny side up.

JIMMY: Sunny side Yuki man.

YUKI: Dip my toast in them eggs.

JIMMY: Sloppy mess.

YUKI: Gooey yum.

JIMMY: You're a freak and a half, you know that?

YUKI: 'Cuz I like eggs?

JIMMY: 'Cuz you're all sunny side drippity drip down the side of the plate, that's why.

YUKI: 'Least I know what I like.

JIMMY: Strange *manga* shit.

YUKI: Huh?

JIMMY: Like, sunny side ain't even Japanese, bro.

YUKI: Who says I'm Japanese?

JIMMY: Well, your family-

YUKI: Born here. Just like me. Hell, I got Mexican, Indian and God knows what else in my blood.

JIMMY: All American mutt.

YUKI: Hell yeah! Not like we live in Iceland.

JIMMY: How's that?

YUKI: Y'know. They're all the same there. Same gene pool or somethin.'

JIMMY: That true?

YUKI: What I hear.

JIMMY: That's sick.

YUKI: Mad sick. Strange country. All snow and ice and…

JIMMY: Been?

YUKI: Seen. On the YouTube.

JIMMY: Man, I hate snow.

YUKI: It's a bitch, right?

JIMMY: We visited up north once, got caught right in middle of a snowstorm… I was never so cold in my life. Snow up to my knees.

YUKI: Yeh?

JIMMY: Had to put my feet in warm water as soon as we made it to the hotel. I was shiverin' like a child. Rosalie says I was tearin' up, too. All I remember was being cold 'n scared 'n wantin' to come back home.

YUKI: Lucky here.

JIMMY: Hot as all get, but at least we ain't freezin'.

YUKI: Don't know why my momma named me snow.

JIMMY: Huh?

YUKI: Yuki means snow.

JIMMY: Never knew that.

YUKI: Never asked.

JIMMY: So, what, your name is Snow Skow?

YUKI: Yuki Skow.

JIMMY: But if we go with the meaning-

YUKI: Yeh.

JIMMY: Snow Skow. … it's no wonder…no wonder at all.

YUKI: What?

JIMMY: Clear as day you must've inherited some strange kind of back of the beyond swamp gully gene somewhere.

YUKI: Why you say that?

JIMMY: You like your eggs sunny side up, bro.

YUKI: Look who's talkin' beyond swamp gully. Jimmy of the grits and hash.

JIMMY: Hey. It's either grits or hash. You think I'm into poundage? I was wrestling champ.

YUKI: High school.

JIMMY: And I could still wrestle me one of these lean punk-ass skateboard kids if I had to.

YUKI: Beat them down?

JIMMY: Holy hosanna beatin.' I still got the gift.

YUKI: Fake 'em out?

JIMMY: I had the best fake-out in the league. Remember? Dead cross-eyed stare, then flip. Right on their back. Never seen it comin'.

YUKI: If you say…

JIMMY: Want me to prove it?

YUKI: Jimmy the ace, eh?

JIMMY: Jimmy the tiger.

YUKI: …Man oh man.

JIMMY: What?

YUKI: High school's like… Still don't know how I got through.

JIMMY: Cheated, my friend. Like we all did.

YUKI (*fish on the line?*): … 'Nother yellowfish?

JIMMY: Nah.

YUKI: …Sometimes I dream me a hundred pounder.

JIMMY: Monster fish?

YUKI: Would be nice.

The sun burns. The air is thick.

JIMMY: Blasted sun.
YUKI: Couple more hours, we'll be all right.

Scene Two

Exterior. Day. In the backyard. There's some very simple mismatched garden furniture, some tires, milk crates and assorted miscellaneous junk, and a small cooler with soda cans to one side. Rosalie packs handmade craft flowers into boxes as she prays. The tone of the prayer is pragmatic: a natural accompaniment to her activity.

ROSALIE: Pray we gonna get through the mornin'.
Pray we gonna get through the night.
Lord on high, listen to your people.
'Cuz 'tis not enough to say Lord have mercy
When we got our lives in Your hands.
Lord, deliver us
So that we may see Your light.
Hear us, oh Lord. Hear us.

Jimmy walks in.

JIMMY: Can hear you clear 'cross the street, Rosalie.
Gonna scare the neighbors.
ROSALIE: Scare nobody.

JIMMY: Prayin' like that, gonna scare somebody. Turnin' into a preacher now?

ROSALIE: That put you out?

JIMMY: If I'd known I was gonna shack up with a preacher, I'd have turned east three ways and done some things different.

He caresses her.

ROSALIE: Yeah?

JIMMY *(continues caressing)*: Whole. Lot. Different.

ROSALIE *(playful, sensual)*: You are a case.

JIMMY *(caressing)*: That's why you married me, right?

ROSALIE *(sinking into him)*: Mmm…

JIMMY: Right?

ROSALIE: You are one stinky sonofabitch, mister man.

JIMMY: Thought you liked my stink-ity stink.

ROSALIE: Get you in the shower.

JIMMY: Get you with me? *(more intimate with his caressing)*

ROSALIE: Jimmy…

JIMMY: What?

ROSALIE *(playful)*: Stop.

JIMMY: You started.

ROSALIE: Swear. You're like a child sometimes.

JIMMY *(improvising a tune)*: Rosalie, Rosalie, sweet as a honey bee…

ROSALIE: Mmm.

JIMMY *(continues song)*: Rosalie, Rosalie, you are my cuppa tea.

ROSALIE: Where'd that come from?

JIMMY: Made it up.

ROSALIE: Just like that?

JIMMY: Got all sorts of songs in my head.

ROSALIE: Poet man.

JIMMY *(a caress, more sexual in nature)*: Lover man.

ROSALIE: It's not even supper time yet.

JIMMY: So?

ROSALIE: So, it's not time, all right?

JIMMY *(moving away, improvising tune, as he grabs a soda from cooler)*: Rosalie, Rosalie, stingy as she can be.

ROSALIE: I'm stingy now?

JIMMY *(sips soda, and then)*: … Nothin' like market-brand cola.

ROSALIE: It's cheaper.

JIMMY: Don't taste the same.

ROSALIE: Wanna pay the extra two dollars for "the real thing," go ahead.

JIMMY: Sometimes you save more by not savin.'

ROSALIE: Makes no sense.

JIMMY: Think about it: I gotta drink up two of these to have me the same effect as the brand. Pay less, but spend more. See?

ROSALIE: Shouldn't be downin' cola anyway.

JIMMY: It's burnin'.

ROSALIE: Gonna get all gassy.

JIMMY: I never get gassy.

ROSALIE: Huh.

JIMMY: When? When do I-?

ROSALIE: Church. That time.

JIMMY: Hell. You still gonna rag on me 'bout that? That was, like… years ago.

ROSALIE: …You get yourself any lunch, croonin' man?

JIMMY *(he can't remember)*: Don't know.

ROSALIE: What you mean?

JIMMY: Fries, I guess.

ROSALIE: What fries?

JIMMY *(making it up maybe? Covering for memory loss?)*: Waffle fries over by steak shack.

ROSALIE: Gonna get fat.

JIMMY: See any fat? I'm lean as a board. Can hit me anywhere. Come on.

ROSALIE: Jimmy.

JIMMY: Hit me.

ROSALIE: Outta your mind.

JIMMY: Hit me.

ROSALIE: *light punch.*

JIMMY: What's that?

ROSALIE: Jimmy.

JIMMY: Hard.

ROSALIE: *punches him much harder.*

JIMMY: Christ.

ROSALIE: You said hard.

JIMMY: I gotta be prepped. You don't just hit a man without any prep.

ROSALIE: Sorry.

JIMMY: Again.

ROSALIE: Jimmy.

JIMMY: I'm prepped now.

ROSALIE: *punches him.*

JIMMY: See? See? Jimmy the tiger.

ROSALIE: All right.

JIMMY: … Whatcha doin'?

ROSALIE (*back in activity mode*): Puttin' the flowers away.

JIMMY: Swap meet? Nobody gonna buy 'em.

ROSALIE: Don't know that.

JIMMY: Know what I see.

ROSALIE: Neva said-

JIMMY: Neva will buy anything that's put in front of her. Christ, you're gonna listen to Neva now?

ROSALIE: Used to run her own beauty shop.

JIMMY: And what happened to it?

ROSALIE: Wadn't her fault.

JIMMY: Wasn't Yuki's fault. Don't tell me you're gonna blame him now.

ROSALIE: Not taking sides.

JIMMY: He's been good husband to her. Through all her rehab shit…

ROSALIE: …You don't like Neva. Ever since high school…

JIMMY: What?

ROSALIE: …I gotta put these boxes in the car.

JIMMY: What you talkin'?

ROSALIE: 'Bout what?

JIMMY: Neva and…

ROSALIE: I was there, Jimmy. Or you think I was just lookin' up at the stars, waitin' for some comet to come shootin' down from the sky?

JIMMY: Didn't hook up that much.

ROSALIE: Can't stand that Yuki ended up with her.

She starts to walk away.

JIMMY: What…?
ROSALIE: I'm gonna sell these flowers. We'll get us some grocery money, and you, mister man, are gettin' NONE of it.

Rosalie walks away and puts boxes in the car.
Jimmy is alone. One of the flowers has been left behind. It's fallen perhaps off to one side. It's a jasmine. He picks it up,
admires it.
A moment.
Rosalie walks in, sees him admiring the jasmine.

ROSALIE: Don't smell.
JIMMY: I know.
ROSALIE: So, what you-?
JIMMY: Turned out nice. *(hands her flower)*
ROSALIE: Jasmine. Got nice shape.
JIMMY: Wish I was good like that.
ROSALIE: What you mean?
JIMMY: With my hands.
ROSALIE: Just stuff I picked up. … Any luck down by the water?
JIMMY: …
ROSALIE: Should take that computer job my uncle told you about.
JIMMY: Sit behind a desk all day?
ROSALIE: Uncle said they were hirin.'

JIMMY: Your uncle lives in the city. Wanna pack up all here, get in the car, n start over? Grew up here, Rosie. This what I know.

ROSALIE: Sometimes gotta do what you don't know.

JIMMY: I'm a fisherman, honey. Got no other life.

ROSALIE *(here we go again)*: Everyone in your family.

JIMMY: Every single one. Yeah. You think I wanna let my daddy and my grand-daddy and my grand-daddy before that down? Ain't quittin.'

ROSALIE: Honorable man.

JIMMY: You say it like it's a sin.

ROSALIE: I just-

JIMMY: Can't sit behind some desk. Lookin' at some screen, hurtin' my eyes, gettin' all carpal tunnel.

ROSALIE: Wouldn't have to be like that.

JIMMY: Your uncle's a good man, but…

ROSALIE: Just think…

JIMMY: What?

ROSALIE: We're behind on the mortgage, credit…

JIMMY: I'll talk to them.

ROSALIE: We've been talkin' to them.

JIMMY: I'll talk to them again.

ROSALIE: Sometimes you gotta do somethin' different from what your ol' man done. Shoemaker's son don't have to be a shoemaker's son. Shoemaker's son can be a cab driver.

JIMMY: What kinda logic's that?

ROSALIE: Can't live like this.

JIMMY: Live fine.

ROSALIE: Jimmy.

JIMMY: I come home, you wanna mess up my day?

ROSALIE: No, but-

JIMMY: Want me to end up like cousin Ray in Waxahachie. He's in a city.

ROSALIE: It's not-

JIMMY: Thirty miles outside of Dallas. Dallas is a city.

ROSALIE: Yes, but he's-

JIMMY: He can't even go to work. Stuck in some ammonia-makin' factory for years and-

ROSALIE: What happened to Ray-

JIMMY: I ain't leavin' here. Ain't lettin' those oil pigs put me out of my life.

ROSALIE: … Not all pigs.

JIMMY: Sleep with 'em?

ROSALIE: What?

JIMMY: Defendin' them.

ROSALIE: We got friends who work-

JIMMY: We got "friends" cuttin' us out of our own jobs, not wantin' us to organize, makin' damn sure we're pushed out more and more every day. What the hell are you talkin' about?

ROSALIE: If your daddy was here…

JIMMY: He'd do the same.

A moment.

ROSALIE: Well. … I got swap meet tomorrow.

JIMMY: What time you headin'?

ROSALIE: Early. You know how it is.

JIMMY: Don't like you drivin' out so early.

ROSALIE: Not the first time.

JIMMY: That's a two lane road. Trucks always on there, not lookin' where they're goin.'
ROSALIE: I'll be fine.
JIMMY: Truckers are watchin' porn, honey. You think they're gonna pay attention to the road? They put their porn on and drive.
ROSALIE: Neva come with.
JIMMY: Neva in the car's like no one in the car.
ROSALIE: Ain't that far.
JIMMY: Road's freaky in the mornin'.
ROSALIE: Come with, then.
JIMMY: ... Don't like swap meets.
ROSALIE: You don't wanna see me rackin' it up.
JIMMY: Rackin' what up?
ROSALIE: Sales, baby. Jasmines and buttercups. And Neva's gonna sell some of her vases, too.
JIMMY: Lord have mercy.
ROSALIE: It's a talent.
JIMMY: You cook this scheme up together?
ROSALIE: No scheme.
JIMMY: How much you're askin' them for?
ROSALIE: Flowers? Two dollars.
JIMMY: Each? You best stay home. Leave all them boxes in the car.
ROSALIE: Got no faith.
JIMMY: Got faith. Just not in people. You think people gonna plunk down two dead presidents on some pipe cleaner buttercup?
ROSALIE: You're turnin' into a sour man. (playful) Sour overgrown lump of a thing.
JIMMY: Leave me, then, if you hate me so much.

ROSALIE: …?

JIMMY: Walk on out there with your flowers and your prayers to God in Heaven. See if you'll find some other patient soul that'll take you under.

ROSALIE: What are you talkin'-?

JIMMY: Always raggin' on Jimmy. Raggin' on Jimmy. Like Jimmy ain't there. Like Jimmy out to some party. When all Jimmy do is work and work and try to get the world to make some goddamn sense. When there ain't no sense to be had. No sir. None at all. But all people see is Jimmy's a fool of a man –

ROSALIE *(gently)*: Hey...

JIMMY (CONT): Jimmy don't know how to do nothin'.
Cept fish and bury his head in the water.
Goddamn bury it,
Until all light gone the way of darkness,
The way of no grace.

Jimmy hands and arms start trembling (involuntarily).
Rosalie draws close.

ROSALIE: Hey...

He can't stop trembling.

ROSALIE (CONT): Jimmy?

JIMMY: …

ROSALIE: Jimmy?

Trembling subsides.

ROSALIE: Gotta see a doctor.

JIMMY: … I'm fine. Just long day.

He kisses her lightly.

ROSALIE *(with affection)*: Stinky.

JIMMY: I'm goin'. *(heads to bathroom inside the house)*

ROSALIE: I put the lemon soap out.

JIMMY: How's that?

ROSALIE: Smells nice.

JIMMY *(softly)*: Right.

He goes within.
Rosalie remains. She absently caresses the fake jasmine.

Scene Three

Exterior. Day. By the water. Yuki is fishing. He sings to himself an improvised, old skool r & b tune. He doesn't have a good singing voice, but he sings with passion regardless.

YUKI: Little sun of mine,
Gonna watch you shine;
Deliver us unto the day.
Little light of mine,
Gonna let you in;
And carry us along the way.
Oh, hit me now.

He makes sounds of a bass guitar thumping.

YUKI: Yeah, yeah. Yeah, yeah, yeah.

*He sways to some imagined horn section and bass playing
groove in his head, perhaps humming along with it or
mimicking the sounds of the horn section. Jimmy walks in.*

JIMMY: You keep shakin' that ass, I'm gonna eat it.
YUKI: Fuck off.
JIMMY: Just raggin.' You know me.
YUKI: You're late, man. Where you been? MickeyD's?
JIMMY: Steak shack for me.
YUKI: At this hour?
JIMMY: They got steak and eggs for breakfast. Aussie
style.
YUKI: What's Aussie got to do with anythin'?
JIMMY: Man, don't you know nothin' bout nothin'?
That's what them Aussies eat down under, down
there in Oz. They wake up every mornin' and have
steak 'n eggs for breakfast.
YUKI: Country of felons.
JIMMY: Huh?
YUKI: Historically.
JIMMY: I'd like to go sometime. They got red desert
there. Red bloomin' earth.
YUKI: Freaky.
JIMMY: Freaky as shit but I wanna see it. No snow
there.
YUKI: They got snow.

JIMMY: Seen any pictures of it? I'm telling you, them Aussies got it made. Perfect fuckin' weather and a red earth that speaks to them, speaks to them in tongues.

YUKI: Where'd you get that?

JIMMY: I read. How's the water lookin'?

YUKI: Same ol' same ol'.

JIMMY: Little fish, eh?

YUKI: ... Rosalie and Neva must be sellin' up a storm by now.

JIMMY: Wish the swap meet was near here. Would put my mind at ease.

YUKI: Just two towns over.

JIMMY: Still worry.

YUKI: Man, you are so in love.

JIMMY: ...?

YUKI: "Oh honey this, oh honey that. Oh baby, mister man."

JIMMY: Shut.

YUKI: It's true.

JIMMY: You're the same.

YUKI: Me and Neva? We're like soldiers when we're together. Grunts and smiles, that's all.

JIMMY: ...You two all right?

YUKI: Holdin' on.

JIMMY: Done good.

YUKI: Ain't no saint.

JIMMY: Done real good, Yuki. ... And rehab done her right.

YUKI: One step at a time.

Fish on the line.

JIMMY: Tug at it.

YUKI: Whatcha think I'm-?

JIMMY: Harder. Harder.

YUKI: Jimmy.

JIMMY: Gonna slip away.

YUKI: How long I been-?

JIMMY: It's veerin', Yuki.

YUKI: It's not-

JIMMY: See? Left ya.

YUKI: 'Cuz you're all screamin' in my ear.

JIMMY: Wadn't screamin'.

YUKI: Christ. You gotta watch it sometimes.

JIMMY: What?

YUKI: Micro-managin.'

JIMMY: I don't micro-manage. I was just…

YUKI: …

JIMMY: Sorry.

A moment.

YUKI: Man, you got your head in your ass sometimes.
We needed that fish. Or you win the lottery or
somethin'? … Nothin' but carryin' you along.

JIMMY: What?

YUKI: Every day.

JIMMY: Carryin' me? I been holdin' us down for
months.

YUKI: Huh.

JIMMY: I know this water, Yuki; Know it like it's my
flesh and blood. Always known where we can make.

Where fish come, when they come... Way I see it, I'm
the one who's carryin' you.
YUKI: That right?
JIMMY: When it comes right down to it. Yeh.
YUKI: See the world the way you wanna see it.
JIMMY: See it how it is.
YUKI: Okay.
JIMMY: No, man, you got somethin' to say, say it.
YUKI: ... Long time.
JIMMY: Long time what? Wanna fly solo?
YUKI: Not flyin' anythin', it's just -
JIMMY: I run this show.
YUKI: Jimmy.
JIMMY: I run it. No one else. ... What? You think
different?
YUKI: We ain't made in weeks, man.
JIMMY: We'll make. Fuck. ... We've been years. What
the hell you talkin'? What the hell you talkin' now?
YUKI: ... Fish gone. That's all.

A moment.

JIMMY: What's that?
YUKI: Huh?
JIMMY: Sounds like bugles.
YUKI: Don't hear nothin'.
JIMMY: Listen. ... Hear that?
Sounds like bugles.
YUKI: ... Another protest happenin'.
JIMMY: Where?
YUKI: Down shore.

JIMMY: What kinda protest?

YUKI: Bout people gettin' sick.

JIMMY: People been gettin' sick.

YUKI: More sick. Louie Medina died last night just from swimmin'.

JIMMY: Louie Medina from-?

YUKI: Gas station. Yeh.

JIMMY: Just a kid.

YUKI: Sixteen years old.

JIMMY: Christ. Why didn't you tell me he'd passed?

YUKI: Only found out myself. They say his esophagus disintegrated, and his heart ballooned up.

JIMMY: From swimmin'?

YUKI: Chemical. In the water. … Y'know. The kind they used to disperse the spill…

JIMMY Corexit?

YUKI: All over everythin'.

JIMMY: Not everythin'.

YUKI: How we know?

JIMMY: It'd be, like, orange alert or somethin'.

YUKI: Red and yellow? Fuck that shit. They're fuckin' with us.

JIMMY: Fuckin' with us, but they can't be fuckin' us completely.

YUKI: They're fuckin' us up the ass, Jimmy. And we're fishin', like we got all the time in the world.

JIMMY: Look, I know they don't give a shit 'bout us. But this, this what you're talkin'…

YUKI: Not just me.

JIMMY: Can't. 'Cuz then we'd all be… I mean, you got a baby comin'.

YUKI: Not for a while yet.

JIMMY: But it's comin.' Neva's what? Four months in?

YUKI: Two.

JIMMY: So, it just can't. Gotta be some patch of air, water…

YUKI: All I know is the kid was swimmin' and he died from it.

JIMMY: …Louie Medina. Little Louie Medina. Always stiffin' me at the pump.

YUKI: He was a good kid, Jimmy.

JIMMY: Not sayin' he wasn't.

YUKI: His folks are a wreck.

JIMMY: You talk to them?

YUKI: Paid my respects. As soon as I-

JIMMY: Gotta do that. They're still at the-?

YUKI: Blue house. Yeh.

A moment.

YUKI: What this town come to when a kid like that just…?

JIMMY (*sung to the tune of "Welcome to the Jungle"*): Welcome to the apocalypse.

YUKI: *imitates a guitar riff in response.*

JIMMY: Watch it bring you to your kn-kn-knees.

YUKI (*extemporaneously, within the tune, in response, guitar-like, snarling; perhaps too Jimmy joins him*): I wanna watch you bleed, bleed bleed bleed bleed.

They laugh, perhaps too much. A release of many things.

YUKI: Now, THAT is one old motherfuckin' song.
Jimmy's torso starts to tremble (involuntarily). He can't stop.

YUKI : Hey. Jimmy?

He keeps shaking.

YUKI: What's goin' on, man?

Jimmy continues.

YUKI: Jimmy?

After brief while, it stops. A breath. A moment.

YUKI: Gotta see a doctor. That stuff's serious.
JIMMY: I'll be fine.
YUKI: Not normal, okay?
JIMMY: Look at me.
YUKI: …
JIMMY: Jimmy the tiger, right?
YUKI: … Gotta see one.
JIMMY: Everybody tellin' me what to do.
YUKI: I'm not-
JIMMY: Like I don't know my own mind. I ain't some kid. Shit. Ain't like little Louie Medina.
YUKI *(gently)*: Waste.
JIMMY: … The poor kid passes on… you think Big Pig gonna pay for his burial 'cuz of some protest?

YUKI: Didn't say-

JIMMY: Man, they'll come up with some story says he was on meth or somethin.' Make it so they got nothin' to do with nothin'- like they don't even know what kinda chemical they used.

YUKI: You said it. "Memories like sieves."

JIMMY: Memories like sieves, so we can keep on the keep on. And that poor kid dead. 'Cuz we let 'em.

YUKI: Don't.

JIMMY: You out there protestin'?

YUKI: Don't see you out there.

JIMMY: I'll go. In time.

YUKI: Uh-huh.

JIMMY: I'll go.

YUKI: Day I see it...

A moment.

JIMMY: (*a turn, a vision*) ...Like I can see him in the water.

YUKI: Who?

JIMMY: Louie Medina.

YUKI: Ain't in the water.

JIMMY: Doin' a backstroke. Smilin' at me. With his bandanna on. Still greasy from work.

YUKI: What?

JIMMY: Like he wants to tell me somethin'. With that crooked smile of his.

YUKI: You really see him?

JIMMY: Like he wants to hold my hand.
Like he wants to hold my hand.

YUKI: Quit that.

JIMMY: *(inside the vision)*: Hey. Louie. I'm right here, son.

YUKI: You're freakin' me out.

JIMMY: Go on. Don't be afraid.

This here is warm earth, warm hands, cracklin' of leaves.

YUKI *(softly)*: Jimmy?

JIMMY (CONT): This here is slick rain, strong fingers,

And the pull of earth and fire inside me.

Pull up close. That's right.

Take my hand, son. Take it for all its worth.

We'll all be in water soon.

Scene Four

Exterior. Late day. Jimmy and Rosalie's backyard. Neva walks in from the driveway (unseen). She's worn out, but refuses to give in to fatigue. She carries a box full of vases. She sets the box down. Looks about the yard. A sigh. A premonition?

ROSALIE *(from Off)*: Neva? Those vases set down okay?

NEVA: Yeah. Need any help over there?

ROSALIE *(from Off)*: Almost done.

Neva sits. She lets the hint of a breeze hit her skin. A surrender to something. Perhaps a secret wish? She smiles. A moment. Another sigh. Sweet and full of mystery.

NEVA: Serenity. Beauty. Happiness.
This is what we wish for in life.
This is what we whisper to ourselves
When we wake up in the mornin'.
The words shiver. Shake. They got lives of their own.
They want nothin' to do with us.
But we call them back.
We say "Serenity, Beauty, Happiness. Step in.
Step inside my heart.
Let me be good. Just once."
And the words rest on our tongue
Like they got all the time in the world.
And they answer with Sadness. Pain. Surrender.
And we say thank you.

The air is burning but she feels a sudden chill.

ROSALIE *(from Off)*: I am burnin' up.
NEVA: What?
ROSALIE *(from Off)*: So hot.
NEVA: Yeah.
ROSALIE *(walking in)*: Gonna bake eggs on the
sidewalk if it keeps on. Want a soda?
NEVA: I'm soda'd out. Had about as much as I could
take at the swap meet. Besides, it's not good for the
baby, is it?
ROSALIE: Well, I'm thirsty. *(grabs soda from cooler)*
That was a long drive. *(drinks soda)* Jimmy was right.
NEVA: …?
ROSALIE: Don't taste the same.
NEVA: Market brand is cheaper.

ROSALIE: Like syrup warmed over.
NEVA: Give here.
ROSALIE: Thought you didn't-
NEVA: Last soda for the day.

Rosalie hands her soda can. Neva sips.

NEVA: Too sweet for my blood.
ROSALIE: Don't have to drink it.
NEVA: I'll sip it slow, fight off the heat.
ROSALIE: Best stay out here. Cuz you do NOT want to be inside.
NEVA: Your AC ain't workin'?
ROSALIE: More like no AC.
NEVA: Broke down?
ROSALIE: Had to sell the unit. To cover the bills.
NEVA: 'Least you got a yard. Some folks don't have nothin'.
ROSALIE: When we moved in here, I had all these plans for the yard. Was gonna go all designer on it, plant this n' that, but never got round to it. Every time I sit out here…
NEVA: Not that bad.
ROSALIE: How many times I've asked Jimmy to throw out those ol' tires? Think he listens? He just walks around and forgets about everythin.'
NEVA: He doin' okay?
ROSALIE: Don't know.
NEVA: What you mean?
ROSALIE: He's worryin' me.
NEVA: Worryin' how?

ROSALIE: ... He's gettin' these shaking fits. Gets dizzy sometimes. Headaches and things. Says it's nothin', but...

NEVA: Should go to the doctor.

ROSALIE: How much that gonna cost? We ain't got medical.

NEVA: Don't get at work?

ROSALIE: Part timers don't get benefits. What country you live in?

NEVA: I thought...

ROSALIE: Dream on.

A moment.

NEVA: You know, the clinic's got this walk-in deal. I bet they'd see him.

ROSALIE: He was doin' fine, too. Then these last coupla weeks, it's like some kinda weird plague's come over him. First he got the flu, and then some weird allergy thing. And now these fits from I don't know where.

NEVA: Big fits?

ROSALIE: Gets nauseous and dizzy. And he says his throat's always burnin'.

NEVA: He needs to see a specialist.

ROSALIE: I think if we just left, moved to a city somewhere, everythin' would work itself out somehow.

NEVA: Take him to the clinic. They'll help you work somethin' out.

ROSALIE: He'll never go.

NEVA: If you tell him it's for his own good…
ROSALIE: Opposite. Gotta tell him it's NOT for his own good, then maybe he'll go.
NEVA: That how it is?
ROSALIE: Jimmy's a piece of work.

A moment.

NEVA: You try havin' kids? …Sometimes when men know they're gonna be fathers, they act different. More responsible. Don't you wanna have kids?
ROSALIE: Can't feed ourselves right. How we gonna feed a kid? Hell, we don't even got a pet. Besides, we can't anyway.
NEVA: Can't have [kids]?
ROSALIE: Not any more.
NEVA: Sorry. … At least we made somethin' today.
ROSALIE: Yeh. People liked the jasmines.
NEVA: Orchids too.
ROSALIE: You were hawkin' them like all get. Got a real gift.
NEVA: Just sales.
ROSALIE: Well, you sure know how to do it.
NEVA: 'Cept with my own stuff.
ROSALIE: We'll sell the vases next time.
NEVA: … Made us fifty dollars.
ROSALIE: Enough for gas.
NEVA: More than that.
ROSALIE: Don't know why they keep raisin' the prices at the pump. Won't be able to drive at all, if it keeps up like this.

NEVA: Bicycle.

ROSALIE: How am I gonna do groceries on a bicycle?

NEVA: Corner store.

ROSALIE: Corner store don't got shit, and it's past dated.

NEVA: What you mean?

ROSALIE: You go in there?

NEVA: Milk n' stuff.

ROSALIE: Best check the date. They had a jar of peanut butter that was two months past. Date was clear on the jar too. I said to them: you best take this off the shelf. Know what they said? Nobody notice.

NEVA: Report them.

ROSALIE: Like the FDA is gonna come down here to the corner store and put them outta business.

NEVA: Might.

ROSALIE: Don't give that place another month.

NEVA: ...So hot.

ROSALIE: ... Feel it yet?

NEVA: Baby? Sometimes I think I do. But I could just be dreamin.'

ROSALIE: Boy?

NEVA: Don't know. Yuki and I want it to be a surprise. It was a surprise I was even pregnant to begin with.

ROSALIE: Been tryin', though.

NEVA: Yeah, but we'd stopped tryin' for a while.

ROSALIE: How come?

NEVA: Too much stuff.

ROSALIE: What kind?

NEVA: Girl, you get a man and woman together, you think it can be narrowed down? One thing my momma told me: there's no end (to what can go on) between a man and a woman once you put 'em together. ... So, like, a baby was the farthest thing from...

ROSALIE: But it's good, though.

NEVA: Do what we can. Like you and Jimmy.

ROSALIE: Me and Jimmy what?

NEVA: You know.

ROSALIE: We're fine.

NEVA: Yeh?

ROSALIE: Look, you and Yuki may be havin' problems, but Jimmy and I are fine.

NEVA: As long as he treats you right...

A moment.

ROSALIE: This yard's a mess.

NEVA: It's pretty bad.

ROSALIE *(laughs)*: Awful, right?

NEVA: Want me to help you clean it up a bit?

ROSALIE: You gotta rest, 'cuz of the baby.

NEVA: Girl, you see me balloonin' out yet? I can move around. Been movin' all day hawkin' at the swap meet, right? What you wanna clean up?

ROSALIE: ...Everythin.'

NEVA: How 'bout we start small? Give us somewhere to go? This milk crate?

ROSALIE: Okay.

NEVA: What's all here?

ROSALIE: Jimmy's things.

NEVA: Screwdriver, pack of cards, ol' newspaper, T-shirt. Smells, too.

ROSALIE *(takes T-shirt)*: I'll wash it.

NEVA: Postcards, compass… *(comes upon an item)* What's this?

JIMMY *(walks in)*: Riflin' through my stuff?

ROSALIE: Just cleanin'.

JIMMY: That's my headgear. Leave it be.

NEVA: From wrestlin'?

JIMMY: Got a problem with that?

NEVA: Keep what you want.

ROSALIE: Can't keep everythin'.

JIMMY: Why? You goin' somewhere?

ROSALIE: No, but-

JIMMY: Then what's it matter what I wanna keep or not?

NEVA: You don't wrestle anymore.

JIMMY: Headgear still fits.

ROSALIE *(taking crate away)*: All right.

JIMMY: I said, leave it.

ROSALIE: Just gonna put it inside.

JIMMY: Why?

ROSALIE: 'Cuz what's all this junk doin' out in the yard anyway? Ain't the place for it.

JIMMY: Been. For some time.

ROSALIE: Well, I don't like it. No more.

Rosalie goes into the house. A moment.

JIMMY: You been instigatin' again?

NEVA *(in stride)*: …Hi, Jimmy.

JIMMY: Hey, Neva.

NEVA: Where you leave my Yuki, huh?

JIMMY: He's comin.' Just stopped off at the market. You two make a fortune over at the swap meet?

NEVA: Did all right.

JIMMY: See your vases are still here.

NEVA: Sold some.

JIMMY: Two, three?

NEVA: One.

JIMMY: One's not "some." *(looking at vases in box)* You make these?

NEVA: Collected them. Over time.

JIMMY: You're sayin' these are vases you got from when somebody gave you flowers, that sort of thing?

NEVA: That's right.

JIMMY: People gotta be outta their mind to buy old vases.

NEVA: People sell what they can.

JIMMY: And people buy-

NEVA *(simultaneous)*: What they need.

JIMMY *(simultaneous)*: What they DON'T need, and then go to market n' can't pay for the groceries. That's what I see.

   Jimmy grabs soda from cooler, opens can, drinks: a ritual.

NEVA: You never used to do that.

JIMMY: Huh?

NEVA: Cola.

JIMMY: Drink every day. What you talkin'?

NEVA: Just thinkin' back.

JIMMY: Was in training then.

NEVA: You used to be so… rigorous.

JIMMY: That's a big word.

NEVA: You were.

JIMMY (playful): Well, I sure remember being that with you. We'd get all skuzzy n'-

NEVA: Stop.

JIMMY (continuing): Skinny-dipping in the miracle pond.

NEVA: Jimmy.

JIMMY (continuing): And then we'd cuddle up crude 'n tangly, all arms n legs n tattoos stickin' out, like little firecrackers gonna burn the night up.

NEVA: You done?

JIMMY: Just reminiscin'.

NEVA: Quit.

JIMMY: Things in mind.

NEVA: Give your mind a rest.

JIMMY: You still got that little scar by your-

NEVA: We are NOT goin' back there. All right? You hear me?

JIMMY (playful, with a sense of history): Just ridin' you.

NEVA: Yeah.

JIMMY: It was high school.

NEVA: Well, you were a good wrestler.

JIMMY: Good? I was the best man on the team. This town's never seen another like.

NEVA: Might.

JIMMY: I was hard core. Super-focused.

NEVA: And now?

JIMMY: What?

NEVA: Just askin.'

JIMMY: Askin' what?

NEVA: Nothin.'

JIMMY: You are so fulla shit.

NEVA: Hey.

JIMMY: Goin' round in circles just like the ol' days.

NEVA: No circles here.

JIMMY: Spit it out, Neva. I know you're itchin' to lay it on me.

NEVA: You're wrong.

JIMMY: Okay.

NEVA: Just think-

JIMMY: What?

NEVA: … you're feelin' okay?

JIMMY: Feelin'? Well, Neva, I'm feelin' fine. How 'bout you?

NEVA: Good.

JIMMY: Then we're all good. Right?

He sits, taking in what little breeze there is. A moment. Jimmy's body begins to tremble. Even more intensely this time. His body continues to do so during the following:

NEVA: Should see a doctor.

JIMMY: Just stuff that come over…

NEVA: Ain't stuff to be triflin' with. Lots of people sick and gettin' sick. And you're workin', right there, right on the water.

JIMMY: So's Yuki. And he's fine. Isn't he?

The trembling begins to subside.

JIMMY: You got nothin' to worry 'bout. Rosalie neither. Everythin's easy breezy...this here day.

It stops.

NEVA: You're impossible.
JIMMY *(trying to be playful)*: I'm swag.
NEVA: In those clothes?
JIMMY: This is the new style. Haven't you heard?
NEVA: I mean it 'bout the doctor. If not for your sake, then for Rosalie. She needs you.
JIMMY: Always with the orders.
NEVA: Just being a friend.
ROSALIE *(from Off, from within, calling out window)*: ...That's all right. You can park there.
JIMMY: Must be Yuki.
NEVA: Wonder what he got at market.
ROSALIE *(walks in from house)*: He's parkin' out front. He was all worried about double parkin' and blockin' the neighbor's driveway.
JIMMY: It's not like we're in a residential.
NEVA: Yuki gets all frazzled 'bout parkin'.
ROSALIE: That new?
NEVA: Just a thing of his these days.
YUKI *(walking in)*: Man, I hate double-parkin'. Bites me in the ass. Every single time.
NEVA: Need to practice, honey.
YUKI: Been practicin'. Years. Still can't get it right.
ROSALIE: People here ain't gonna measure whether you're an inch from the curb or a half inch.
YUKI: Pride. That's all. Hurts my pride.

NEVA: Softie.
YUKI: I'm not.
NEVA: Hey.

Neva and Yuki kiss.

JIMMY: Thought you'd left us, bro.
YUKI: Like I'm gonna leave my lady here with you.
JIMMY: I'm harmless.
YUKI: He look harmless to you?
ROSALIE: Not with that face.
JIMMY: What face?
YUKI: Player.
JIMMY: Ain't no player.
NEVA: Not what I heard.
JIMMY: Well, you've been talkin' to some misinformed individuals. 'Cuz this here man ain't played nothin' in a long time.
YUKI: Oh glory Saint Jimmy the divine.
ROSALIE: Hallelujah.
NEVA: Holy be.
JIMMY: Y'all like ridin' me. All right. I can take. 'Cuz I know I'm a good citizen, don't bother nobody.
YUKI: Amen.
JIMMY: You get the Hot Pockets on?
ROSALIE: They're done.
JIMMY: Well, hell, baby, bring them out. I'm starvin'.
ROSALIE: Only put two on.
JIMMY: Put two more.
ROSALIE: Don't got two more.

JIMMY: What you mean? We did groceries two days ago.

ROSALIE: I just buy for the week, Jimmy. Exact count. You know that.

NEVA: Don't worry. We ate a bit at the swap meet.

JIMMY: You bought things?

ROSALIE: Hot chips.

NEVA: I was cravin'.

JIMMY *(to Yuki)*: She's already in cravin' mode?

NEVA: Not that much.

YUKI: What time I had to get up last night 'cuz you wanted curly fries?

NEVA: One night.

YUKI: And another and another.

NEVA: You tell your story, I'll tell mine. Go on, Jimmy. Have your Hot Pocket. We don't need. Yuki brought stuff, right?

YUKI: Huh?

NEVA: Didn't you go to the market?

YUKI: No.

NEVA *(to Jimmy)*: Thought you said-

JIMMY: Thought he did. Isn't that what you said, Yuki?

YUKI: Well…

ROSALIE: I have some popcorn I could bring out.

NEVA: We gotta get goin' anyway.

YUKI: Just got here.

NEVA: Well, we can't stay here all night, Yuki.

YUKI: Not even twilight yet.

NEVA: What's that got to do with anythin'?

YUKI: I like seein' the twilight from this yard. They got a nice view here. Can really see the green ray.
NEVA: Huh?
YUKI: Just as sunset hits...
ROSALIE: Or sunrise...
JIMMY: Flash of green.
NEVA: Don't think I've ever seen it.
ROSALIE: Sure you have. Every time the sun's about to come up or about to rest...right against the horizon line...green ray. My auntie used to say you could wish on it.
NEVA: Yeah?
YUKI: They got the best view here.
NEVA: We got a view.
YUKI: What view?
NEVA: All right. *(playful)* So, where'd you go, private eye?
YUKI: Hmm?
NEVA: If you didn't go to market.
YUKI: Went down to the protest.
JIMMY: Did what?
YUKI: Over by the big tanker.
ROSALIE: What protest?
YUKI: Jimmy didn't tell you?
ROSALIE: Didn't tell us a thing.
YUKI: Louie Medina died.
ROSALIE: Gas station kid?
YUKI: Yep.
ROSALIE: Don't tell me he OD'd. Can't bear to think another kid in this town-
YUKI: Nothin' like that.

NEVA: What, then?

JIMMY: Swimmin'.

YUKI: He didn't die from-

JIMMY: He died from swimmin'; the water's contaminated.

ROSALIE: Contaminated with what?

YUKI: Chemical. Y'know, that Corexit thing they used to disperse the spill.

NEVA: Louie was such a sweet kid.

ROSALIE: I should take his folks a pie or somethin'.

JIMMY: What's that gonna do? Pie ain't gonna bring him back.

ROSALIE: Well, sometimes all you can do is…

NEVA (*a shared sense of history*): Make somethin'.

ROSALIE: Yeah.

JIMMY: Won't do any good.

ROSALIE: Jimmy.

JIMMY: No pie on earth could bring my daddy back. … Neva knows what I'm talkin'.

NEVA: That was a long time…

JIMMY: House filled with pies. Remember? Christ. The stink…

ROSALIE: Well, what do you want me to do? Walk by Louie Medina's folks' house, n do nothin'?

NEVA: We'll take somethin' over to them later.

ROSALIE: All right.

NEVA: Was it a big protest, honey?

YUKI: Pretty fierce. Didn't want to leave. We were all chantin' n wavin', holdin' up signs. Felt good to feel like I was doin' somethin' for a change.

NEVA: You do things.

YUKI: Sign petitions. Yeh. But not like this. Not like really doin' somethin'.

JIMMY: Huh.

YUKI: It's true. Like, if there'd been a protest when your cousin Ray was in that factory fire in Waxahachie. Wouldn't you have wanted to be there?

JIMMY: But there wadn't no protest.

YUKI: Hypothetical.

JIMMY: Hypothetical don't count.

YUKI: Always micro-managin.'

JIMMY: How am I micro-managin'? Somethin' real and somethin' hypothetical is not the same thing, Yuki.

ROSALIE: We should go down there.

JIMMY: Raise our hands, shout?

NEVA: Yuki's right. If it was your cousin-

JIMMY: I'd be there. If in REALITY, there'd been a protest up in Waxahachie. 'Cuz it's regardin' a solvable problem. A containable problem.

YUKI: This ain't?

JIMMY: This is different.

ROSALIE: I don't see what's different about it.

JIMMY: Honey, all I'm sayin' is what we got here, this what-the-what thing, is a helluva lot different than some factory fire in Waxahachie.

YUKI: Accountability is accountability.

NEVA: Maybe Jimmy just wants to think about it.

JIMMY: Been thinkin' about it. Days and days, as the days roll on the days.

YUKI: So, what? You think I'm an ass for going down there?

JIMMY: Didn't say-

YUKI: You're implyin.'

JIMMY: World moves the way it moves, Yuki.

YUKI: And we just swim in its current? Even if we're fucked.

JIMMY: We're already fucked.

ROSALIE: What's got into you? You were all Mister resistance man Che Guevara n' Bob Marley T-shirt in high school.

YUKI: Rage against the machine, bro.

JIMMY: Still am.

YUKI: Don't see it.

JIMMY: I rage when the provenance of rage demands it.

YUKI: What the fuck is that?

NEVA: I think what Jimmy means is-

JIMMY: How you know what I mean, Neva? You inside my brain all of a sudden? All creepy crawlin'?

NEVA: Just meant-

JIMMY: Don't know nothin'. ... I go, if I go, when I'm good n' ready. Just not now.

ROSALIE: Chickenin' out.

JIMMY: Not chickenin' anythin.' But I just don't see what good's it gonna do now to shout n make signs n, n...

He stutters. Intimations of a very slight fit accompanied by dizziness.

ROSALIE: Jimmy?

JIMMY (*trying to complete thought*): When there's...

ROSALIE: Want some [cola]?
JIMMY: No.

He reorients himself, continues his thought:

JIMMY (CONT): When they got their minds... fixed anyway.
ROSALIE: Don't know that. There are people who work there-
JIMMY Don't you go on now with that "friends" crap.
ROSALIE I'm not-
JIMMY: We got two, two so-called friends, Bailey and whatshisface...
ROSALIE: Arthur.
JIMMY (CONT): Arthur. Who work over there at the Big Pig, and they didn't even say as much a "good mornin'" when we passed them by on our way to church on Sunday.
ROSALIE: Didn't see us.
JIMMY: They don't wanna see us. Which is a different thing altogether. Why do you think they sprayed the fuckin' chemical all over? You think if we were all rich here, they'd been so careless with that thing?
YUKI: Were you at the protest?
JIMMY: Don't have to be to know.
YUKI: Same ol fuckin' shit.
JIMMY: How's that?
YUKI: Talk the talk, but I don't see you walkin'.
JIMMY: And you are?
YUKI: Yeah, man. I am.
NEVA *(trying to calm him down)*: Honey.

YUKI: It's true, Neva. All this time, I been tryin' to lay low, carry on. And what it'd do? Shit still goes on. Can't keep pretendin' it don't. So, I go, yeah, and I'm gonna keep goin', n protest as much as I can.

JIMMY: Gonna change their mind?

YUKI: I figure… with this kid dyin'…

JIMMY: Man, as long as the profit margin goes up on their end, Big Pig don't care WHAT.

ROSALIE: Plenty reason, then, to go down there and…

JIMMY: I chain myself to some tanker, right now, chain myself like some warrior hero, will that make them do things different? The water's already poisoned.

NEVA: Not all of it.

JIMMY: The lesser and the minor ain't the cause here.

NEVA: What you mean?

ROSALIE: I think tests gotta be run. Thorough tests.

JIMMY: On whose demands?

ROSALIE: Our demands. We live here. We count for somethin'.

JIMMY: Don't know a thing…

ROSALIE: I'll talk to Bailey and-

JIMMY: Don't go messin' about, stirrin' up a goddamn fuss.

ROSALIE: I'll do what I like.

JIMMY: Just gonna get us deeper and deeper-

ROSALIE: We're already in the shit, Jimmy. Can't get much deeper.

JIMMY: What you-?

ROSALIE: You think we're doin' okay? I got popcorn and Hot Pockets in the house. That the way you wanna live? And when I gotta take you to the doctor, how is that gonna work out? Huh?

JIMMY: What doctor?

ROSALIE: Know full well.

JIMMY: Told you. Ain't goin'.

YUKI: Jimmy, you gotta-

JIMMY: So they can charge me up the ass for stuff I ain't got. No sir. My daddy gone through all that. I'm not goin.'

ROSALIE: That was different.

JIMMY: Different time. Yeh. Same doctors.

NEVA: Look, I think what Jimmy means is that we gotta wait, see what gives.

ROSALIE: Don't play Miss Protocol and Understandin', Neva. I know you.

NEVA: What is that supposed to mean?

YUKI: Look, I think what we need to do here is put things in perspective.

ROSALIE: We gotta make them do some thorough tests, that's all. I'll talk to folks at church.

JIMMY: Send prayers up?

ROSALIE: We go there, make them figure it out. We have a right.

JIMMY: And they'll pay someone to lie for them. On their honor. And we'll still be fucked.

ROSALIE: Then we'll ask someone to do some other tests.

JIMMY: And spend our whole lives lookin' for a particle of truth. That what you want, Rosalie?

ROSALIE: I just think-

JIMMY: Think n think n think. And in the end, what? The big parade goes on like we ain't ever been.

ROSALIE: ...It's not like that.

JIMMY: How you know what it's like? How you goddamn know what anything's like about anythin' round here? I didn't come from some other little town like you, Rosie. Been here my whole life. I know whatever the fuck's gone down and been goin' down.

NEVA: Calm down, Jimmy.

JIMMY: Don't you be orderin' me. I know what I'm sayin'.

YUKI: Look, we ain't said... It's just-

JIMMY: Fuckin' truth and protest? That what you think this is, bro? Truth shine a little light? Little fuckin' light of mine? Man, you got to be kiddin' me. You all gotta be...

Jimmy's whole body starts to tremble. It continues during and through the following...

ROSALIE: Jimmy...

JIMMY *(towards revelation)*: I see it. I fuckin' see...
A dream of water
Hot
Burnin'
Lettin' itself through me
Floatin'
Through the sludge of sticky crude on cane
Down, down the way of no life
ROSALIE: Jimmy?

JIMMY: N this dream, it speaks to me
Speaks to me in tongues,
N it says:
All we got, all we got, all we got, all we got
In this world
Is to go on,
Gettin' up in the mornin'
Doin what we do, fishin' how we can,
Lettin' each day go by, honorin' the past,

Breath. Breath.

As the vultures circle the skies
N the bodies of dead baby dolphins
Wash up along the shore,
Silver, blue, black n torn,
Sweet howlin' babies
Claimed by no one.

Like us, we'll say,
Just like us,
As we look at their vacant eyes
N take each other by the hand
N lie down next to the dolphins
While the vultures peck at our carcasses
N the dolphin skin becomes our own.
Breath. Breath.
N in that moment,
In that moment,
As we're lying there,
With our eyes lookin' up at the sun,

We'll know,
We'll know the water's right.
'Cuz it gives us a kind of peace,
And the promise,
The promise of that... peace

Breath.
Will make us smile as wide as the sun,
In praise and all glory
To the vanishing air.

Jimmy vomits fish from his mouth,
While the others only see blood and bile.

PART TWO:
Scene Five

Exterior. Dawn. In the back
yard. Some time later. A fortnight or so. The backyard has
been stripped of whatever junk was in it. Only the
mismatched garden furniture, the small cooler, and a
cardboard sign, face down on the ground, off to one side,
remain. Rosalie sits. She makes an orchid out of pipe
cleaners and whatever else she has in her crafts kit.

ROSALIE: In the evenin' we'd sit, and make beauty.
Hours would go by,
as we picked out this color n' that,
This ribbon and bow,
This appliqué that could go
ROSALIE: Oh so well on our old T-shirt.

Dress-up, we'd call it. Dress-up time.
'Cuz we knew that's all we had.
TV wadn't workin' right. Computer was too old,
And everythin' else was either drinkin', doin' pot,
or hangin' out at the Grab N' Go.
My girlfriends used to say:
"Girl, you're gonna be some kind of artist."
I'd listen to them, and think "They're crazy."
But deep down it felt nice to think maybe…

Some people think pretty things are stupid,
That there's no reason for them to be in this world.
They all: "That crap is just gonna get dusty n' old
And you ain't even gonna be able to get
two cents for it."
But I don't know.
I think if somethin' pretty gets made,
If you devote yourself to it somehow,
Put your soul in it,
And not treat it like work or busy-ness,
It will last. Even if it gets dusty and old.
Even if gets so bent outta shape
You can't even recognize it
twenty-odd years down the line.
As long as you know that in that moment,
The moment it was made,
The person makin' it had belief,
some kind of pure faith,
That's all right.

She finishes the orchid, admires it. Neva walks in.

NEVA: Still out here?

ROSALIE: Got to cleanin'...didn't wanna go back in the house.

NEVA (*looks at orchid, and then deliberately says*): Dragonfly?

ROSALIE: Orchid. Don't you know your flowers? Orchids are the one of the wonders of the earth.

NEVA (*enjoying the game*): Seven wonders, eh?

ROSALIE: Wonders. Didn't say seven wonders.

NEVA: Well...

ROSALIE: Pretty, right?

NEVA: Beautiful. ... You headin' down to the protest later?

ROSALIE: Made a sign. (*points*)

NEVA (*looks about, sees cardboard, walks to it, turns it over, reads*): "Listen to the people's wrath."

ROSALIE: What?

NEVA: Bit Biblical.

ROSALIE: It's true.

NEVA: ... Most people don't even know what "wrath" means.

ROSALIE: It's in the Bible.

NEVA: Yeah, but... Walkin' round the street. You ask somebody flat-out. They'd have no idea what you're talkin' about.

ROSALIE: I'll make new sign, then.

NEVA: Thought you were gonna talk to them, Bailey and whatshisface...

ROSALIE: I will. Soon as Jimmy get out of hospital.

NEVA: Get out today.

ROSALIE: Later. Yeh. Don't what I'm gonna do with him in the house.

NEVA: …?

ROSALIE: How am I gonna take care of him?

NEVA: Can't stay in the hospital…

ROSALIE: I know. But… How am I gonna…? Doctor says his insides are all messed up.

NEVA: Messed up how?

ROSALIE: Real messed up. I keep thinkin' he's got what his daddy got: Cancer. It spread all over his body. Don't wanna see that happen to Jimmy.

NEVA: Won't.

ROSALIE: Ain't a machine. People break down, Neva.

NEVA: Yeh, but…

ROSALIE: And what if I get sick too?

NEVA: You're fine.

ROSALIE: We're ALL exposed to whatever-the-hell-this-is in the air and water. You got that rash that-?

NEVA: Went away.

ROSALIE: For good? … That's what I mean. We don't know WHAT. I could get sick. And then it'd be the two of us hobblin' around with our ailments. That ain't supposed to happen, you know. Not 'til we're old. Not 'til we're at that stage where we just keel off from natural causes.

NEVA: Nobody dies from natural causes anymore.

ROSALIE: Just one sickness after another.

NEVA: Won't get sick.

ROSALIE: I'm not a machine. Everybody thinks I am. "Oh, Rosalie gonna be there. Rosalie gonna carry on just fine." Nobody thinks somethin' could happen to Rosalie. Well, I feel things too. Get so sometimes I can't get up in the mornin' my chest is burnin' up so bad. ... Nobody thinks about that.

A moment.

NEVA: How long does Jimmy got? Doctor tell you?
ROSALIE: A month, a week. Or he could go on, dyin' a little bit …

A moment, then Rosalie rises with orchid in hand. She walks away, in direction of the house. She stops, lost for a moment.

NEVA: Where you goin'?
ROSALIE: …?
NEVA: Goin' back into the house?
ROSALIE: Huh?
NEVA: Whatcha doin', girl?
ROSALIE: I was…

She's lost.

NEVA: Give me that.
ROSALIE: Huh?
NEVA: Orchid.
ROSALIE: *does so.*
NEVA: I'll set it down here. Jimmy come home, he'll see it. Right?
ROSALIE: Pretty.

NEVA: Come on.

ROSALIE: What?

NEVA: Sit yourself down.

ROSALIE: Got all these things to do.

NEVA: Do 'em later. Day's too nice to waste.

ROSALIE: …Clearest sky you ever seen. Woke up this morning, thought I was in some movie show.

NEVA: 3D sky. Yeh.

ROSALIE: Blue as all get.

NEVA: Yard looks nice.

ROSALIE: Cleaned up. Had to.

NEVA: …Can't stop thinkin' about it.

ROSALIE: …?

NEVA: Jimmy… when he started retchin' like that. Blood of angels, I thought. Like the blood of angels comin' out of his mouth.

ROSALIE: Doctor says everythin' inside him is corroded. Like it'd been burnt through crisp as firepaper. Said somethin' about PAH traces in his bloodstream. *(recalling the exact name with care)*: Polycyclic aromatic hydrocarbons.

NEVA: What the hell?

ROSALIE: That's what I said. But doctor was, like, it was perfectly normal everyday thing. Ain't normal. Nothin' about any of this shit goin' down here is normal. And he's all actin' like I ain't supposed to question, ain't supposed to even get angry.

NEVA: Talk to Bailey and whatshisface over at Big Pig.

ROSALIE: Got a mind to all right. Thing is, all they could do is draft a memo or somethin'.

NEVA: Then, sue their fucking ass!

ROSALIE: Sue 'em til they bleed?

NEVA: Do it. Take those bastards to task.

ROSALIE: With what? They cut my hours at work. From part time to some time. That's where I'm at.

NEVA: When'd they-?

ROSALIE: Yesterday. I was, like, shit. What the hell we gonna do now? I ain't even got twenty hours a week I can count on for grocery money and electric. And I got Jimmy in hospital when we ain't got any proper medical to speak of. Who's gonna pay that bill? ...And if I hire me a lawyer on top of that to sue their yellow-belly ass, how's that gonna work out? Lawyer gonna do it for free?

NEVA: I know somebody--

ROSALIE: And how lawyer gonna prove anythin'? Huh? P.A.H just roll around in the air like you can catch it? ... Spend time and hope on some lawsuit, sit in court for how many years, and at the end of the day, you're further in the hole than when you started. Like everyone else 'round here that's tried to do somethin' bout anythin'.

NEVA: But in time...

ROSALIE: When I'm dead?

NEVA: Don't.

ROSALIE: I just wanna go down there to the protest, hold up my sign, breathe, shout, call them "cheap as hooker motherfuckers," and come back home, while we still got it.

NEVA: Ain't gonna lose...

ROSALIE: Yes, we are.

NEVA: Rosie…

ROSALIE: We've been behind on the mortgage how long? Why you think I clean up? Not just 'cuz I had to. … They're gonna lock us outta here pretty soon, and then it'll just me and Jimmy in the car for a while.

NEVA: Stay with us.

ROSALIE: Like you got room.

NEVA: Got spare room.

ROSALIE: Closet?

NEVA: Not a closet.

ROSALIE: Is this the same room I-?

NEVA: Yeh.

ROSALIE: Girl, that's a closet.

NEVA: Well, it's gonna be the baby's room, once we fix it up.

ROSALIE: Air it out, then. Poor baby's gonna get claustrophobic.

NEVA: Babies don't get claustrophobic.

ROSALIE: How you know?

NEVA: If you don't wanna stay in our house…

ROSALIE: Didn't say that.

NEVA: Ain't being enthusiastic.

ROSALIE: Look, time come, we'll figure it out.

NEVA: …How many months you behind on the-?

ROSALIE: Three.

NEVA: Girl, they ain't shut you down yet?

ROSALIE: Jimmy went down to the bank, before all this hospital mess, n' pleaded our case.

NEVA: Must've pleaded real good, put on quite a show.

ROSALIE: Just spoke truth.

NEVA: That worked? … Jimmy's somethin'.

ROSALIE: Pisses me off.

NEVA: Like all men.

ROSALIE: Guys, girls, when people piss you off, they piss you off.

NEVA: Not the same.

ROSALIE: What? You pissed at Yuki? … Is he actin' out?

NEVA: No.

ROSALIE: Don't let him act out.

NEVA: Nothin' like that.

ROSALIE: When guys get violent…

NEVA: He's not violent. Just… I don't know… Everythin', I suppose. I mean, no matter how much Yuki goes down there and protests, and he goes just about every day now,

ROSALIE: That's good.

NEVA: Yeh, it's good, but everybody around here is sick or gonna be.

ROSALIE: Not everybody.

NEVA: How we know? Look at that poor kid Louie Medina. I stood there as they lay his body in the ground.

ROSALIE: Such a sad day.

NEVA: And I thought "that could be any one of us." I mean, I don't wanna think it, - I can't stand to think it - but it's there, y'know. Every time I wake up. Pisses me off.

ROSALIE: Cool down.

NEVA: Tryin'. But I keep thinkin' 'bout the baby – how's it come into this world?

ROSALIE: Like we all done.

NEVA: Had this weird blister on my skin, wouldn't go away. I kept lookin' at it, thinkin' the baby was gonna come out full of blisters too. *(fighting tears, not giving in)*

ROSALIE: Hey.

NEVA: Want to do things right, you know. I wanna have this baby. But... I don't know.

ROSALIE: Come 'ere.

NEVA: Things get so mixed up.

ROSALIE: I know.

They lean on each other. Perhaps an embrace. And then...

NEVA: I think animals are better than us sometimes.

ROSALIE: ...?

NEVA: You think about how many murders people commit, how many wars n invasions n shit, n all this callousness n messed-up-ness we got here... Ought to be ashamed.

ROSALIE: ...Jimmy's got shame. Inside him.

NEVA: What about?

ROSALIE: Never known.

NEVA: Girl, you been together how long?

ROSALIE: Doesn't mean I know him. You know Yuki?

NEVA: THINK I know him.

ROSALIE: Thinkin's not the same as...

NEVA: Not sure I wanna know him.

ROSALIE: Scared?

NEVA: How goddamn awful would it be to really know somebody deep down, like, all their little secrets and desires and darkness? It'd be creepy, right? I know enough. Enough to live a life. Make plans.

ROSALIE: And buy baby things.

NEVA: It's too early.

ROSALIE: Gotta be ready, Neva. Could be a preemie.

NEVA: Nah. Everyone on my side of the family are big ass, fat full term babies. Not a preemie in the bunch.

ROSALIE: I was. Momma said I almost didn't make it I was so little and weak. Went through hell. All those nights in the hospital, waitin' and waitin'. ... Hate waitin' in hospitals. So damn cold. Like iceboxes in there.

NEVA: They keep 'em like that to be hygienic.

ROSALIE: I was, like, I need me a sweater. Shoulda brought one. That blue one Jimmy bought me at Target when we went all the way out there that one time. He picked it out special. I was, like, "Jimmy, it's too much. You can't spend all that on that. And he was, like, I'm gettin' it. For you." And he leaned over and kissed me right in the middle of that store, like we were in high school all over again.

Rosalie is near tears. She may let herself release. A bit.

NEVA: Jimmy will pull through. You'll see.

ROSALIE: With his insides being how they are...

NEVA: ...Some people pull through. Jimmy the tiger, right?
ROSALIE (*recalling cheer*): ..."Rock 'em tiger, do your thing. Jimmy's gonna slam your..."
NEVA (*chant-whoop-cheer*): Make 'em bleeeeed, super-tiiii-ger!

They laugh.

ROSALIE: We were crazy.
NVEA: I always thought Jimmy was gonna go to college with his wrestlin'.
ROSALIE: We got married.
NEVA: Still coulda gone.
ROSALIE: Thought I was gonna have a baby.
NEVA: Didn't know.
ROSALIE: ...
NEVA: ... You two are good together.
ROSALIE: *laughs.*
NEVA: What?
ROSALIE: *keeps laughing.*
NEVA: What's so funny?
ROSALIE: I kept his headgear.
NEVA: What?
ROSALIE: Memento.

Rosalie laughs even more. They both laugh. And then a brief, shared silence.

ROSALIE: Remember when my momma moved us to this town.

I was screamin' in the car, all the way.
I didn't wanna leave our place.
I had everything there.
And auntie, who was with us on the drive, said to me
"You never have everything in one place, child."
Said it, weird like that. With a little smile.
I thought this woman's crazy.
I am going to live in some crazy, crazy place.
I was so scared.
Momma kept drivin'.
The road seemed like it took forever,
Even though it was only a couple of hours.
The closer we got here,
the warmer and less familiar it became.
Hot. Achin.' I wanted to take all my clothes off.
I remember Momma yellin' at me from the front [of
the car]
"Rosalie, put your T-shirt back on.
This is no place to show your boobies."
I laughed. Hysterical.
'Cuz I didn't have any boobies. I was a little girl.
She focused on the drive.
I let the warm breeze hit my skin.
Everythin' in the air was salty,
And smelled of old movies n scratchy vinyl
n primeval stuff.
I stuck my hand out of the car,
n let the heat flood me for a while.
There was the smell of all kinds of fish.
Thought I'd puke.
"Let me out," I cried.

But auntie held me, looked me in the eye, and said
"We're gonna make things here. Don't cry.
We're gonna make all kinds of beautiful things."
And I said "yeah."

Scene Six

*Exterior. Late day. In the backyard. There's a strange kind
of silence that's settled over everything. An odd hum in the
air.
And then: the sound of birds squawking, chasing each
other, fighting over prey?
And then, nothing.
For a little while.*

*The cardboard protest sign is still on the ground, off to one
side. The cooler is open. It may have been opened several
hours ago. Someone forgot to close it.*

*Hazy sun falls across the shapes of the mismatched garden
furniture, as if it were caressing them gently with its rays.
The fake orchid is resting on the garden table. It's been left
behind, forgotten somehow, in the rush to leave.*

*The sun drapes itself across the orchid. A strange kind of
glow.
Only for a moment.
Then it moves on.*

*Jimmy walks in. He looks beat. Out of sorts. Disoriented.
He's trying not to give in.*

He surveys the yard. It's so clean. Stripped of everything.
He can hardly recognize it.
He retches.

A moment.

He wipes his mouth with an old handkerchief that he keeps
in his pocket.
He stands up straight. Breathes.
He sees the orchid on the table. A smile. He walks over to it.
He picks it up.
He shakes. He can't stop. The orchid falls.
He tries to pick it up. But his body fails him.
And then, he stops shaking.
He's fine. He'll be fine.

He sees the sign on the ground. He turns it over. He
laughs. Not mockingly.
What a fucking sign.

He picks it up, holds it in his hands. He raises it up, as if
he were at the protest.
LISTEN TO THE PEOPLE'S WRATH.

He makes a sound, as he holds up the sign. Perhaps a
holler? A shout?
Anger swells up in him.
He throws the sign to the ground. Fucking waste of time.
He remembers some wrestling moves.
Yeah. That's what needs to be done.

He executes them. Pushing his body, pushing everything
inside him.
He will not, will not break…
He retches. Again.

Goddamn.

He wipes his face with the same old handkerchief. The
handkerchief smells. Of vomit, stink…
He hates his body. Hates everything. He kicks the sign.
It's cardboard. It doesn't move very far. It barely moves at
all.
He laughs. Fucking insane. Huge laugh. Says:

JIMMY: Iceland.

Long laugh.

Goddamn.

He sits. Resting. Takes in the sun.
What a day.

A moment.

The hum of a car. Weird hum. Bad motor. Bad sound.
Voices are heard:

ROSALIE (*from off*): I told him to stay in the car-
YUKI (*from off*): Don't understand why he wanted to
walk. That's fuckin' crazy. In his condition.

Jimmy listens.

NEVA *(from off)*: Just wanted some air.
YUKI *(from off)*: What air? It's like an oven today. No air to be found. And sticky as shit. Goddamn irresponsible that you let him walk out like that.
ROSALIE *(from off)*: I am not irresponsible.
YUKI *(from off)*: Indulging him.

Jimmy laughs.

ROSALIE *(from off)*: Man stuck in hospital all this time. I understand he wants air. Poisoned, sticky, what all, but it's understandable. Now, you gonna help me with this shit or what?

Jimmy stretches. His body aches. He coughs a bit.

NEVA *(from off)*: I got it.
ROSALIE *(from off)*: Hold it steady now. Don't want it drippin' all over.
NEVA *(from off)*: Hush puppies don't drip.
ROSALIE *(from off)*: Sauce does.

They walk in.
Rosalie has a grocery store-bought flower arrangement in hand, perhaps accompanied by a balloon that reads "Welcome Back." The balloon, if there, should seem very much out of place. Un-naturally cheery.
Yuki has a convenience store bag: six-pack or so of beer.

Neva has a bag of chain store-bought hush puppies and fish tenders and such.

YUKI: What the hell you doin' here?
JIMMY: Live here.
NEVA: Thought you'd still be out there walkin'.

Rosalie sets flower arrangement down. The others follow suit with their items.

JIMMY: Wanderin' the earth?
ROSALIE: Good to walk, right?

Light kiss between Rosalie and Jimmy.

JIMMY: Hot.
YUKI: We got beer.
NEVA: And hush puppies and fish fingers and little bitty nuggets.
JIMMY: Kiddie food?
ROSALIE: Ain't kiddie food.
JIMMY: Can't eat that.
NEVA: 'Course you can.
JIMMY: Can't eat fried stuff. They shot me up with medicine all over.
ROSALIE: One bite.
JIMMY: No bite. *(referring to sickness)* I'm gonna lick this thing. *(Then to Yuki)* Gimme a beer.
ROSALIE: Jimmy.
JIMMY: It's hot.
NEVA: Shouldn't.

JIMMY: Always with the orders.

NEVA: When do I-?

JIMMY: Ever since way back, you've loved bossin' people around. Am I right or am I right, Yuki?

YUKI: Neva does what she does.

NEVA: I say one thing, one word, and y'all start-

ROSALIE: It's the truth. You love bossin'.

NEVA: Name me one example. Bet you can't.

JIMMY: That time. The amusement park.

NEVA: That was NOT my fault. Those kids were holdin' up the line.

ROSALIE: And at church?

NEVA: I never-

ROSALIE: When the preacher called out his healin' and you were in middle of that argument with that ol' lady?

NEVA: First of all, that lady was rude. Plain rude. She was makin' us ALL uncomfortable. Somebody had to tell her off.

YUKI: And at the store other day? You deliberately asked the manager to re-do that aisle.

NEVA: Cuz it was a hazard, the way it was set up, all crunched up like that. That was a fire hazard. I was doin' 'im a favor. Can you imagine if he'd gotten a citation from the fire department? They'd have shut that place down.

JIMMY: You like bossin.'

NEVA: I like order. Not the same as givin' orders. I think if someone's right out of hospital, they shouldn't be drinkin.'

JIMMY: You should know.

NEVA: Don't you start, Jimmy. All right? Don't you start now.

JIMMY: Hey, I'm just gonna have one beer. That's all.

NEVA: Still shouldn't. Back me up on this one, Rosalie. Don't just stand there.

ROSALIE: He really shouldn't.

JIMMY: Both of you gangin' up on me, eh?

YUKI: For your own good, Jimmy.

JIMMY: I've been cooped up in that place how long, folks pokin' at my insides, hell, I deserve a beer. One beer can't hurt. Got hops in it, right? Hops are natural.

YUKI: Man oh man.

JIMMY: Man oh man what?

YUKI: Nothin', Jimmy. Just man oh man.

Jimmy pops open the can, drinks.

JIMMY: Like I'm some moron.

YUKI: Never said…

JIMMY: Lookin' at me like I am.

YUKI: Ain't lookin' nothin.'

JIMMY: Lookin' all sideways.

YUKI: Just eatin', Jimmy. *(rallying)* Welcomin' you back home, right?

NEVA *(simultaneous)*: Welcome home, Jimmy.

ROSALIE *(simultaneous)*: Welcome home, baby.

JIMMY: ….Ain't been off to war or nothin'.

NEVA: Well. You know.

They eat. A moment.

NEVA: How [are] the hush puppies?
YUKI: They're good.
NEVA: Special recipe.
YUKI: Is that right?
NEVA: That's what the sign said.
YUKI: Probably the sauce.
ROSALIE: It's always the sauce, isn't it?
JIMMY: How's that?
ROSALIE: Always some special ingredient in the sauce. That's how they keep it secret.
JIMMY: That don't make sense.
ROSALIE: It's easier to hide an ingredient in a sauce than it is on a body.
JIMMY: Huh?
ROSALIE: Body of the meat: chicken, steak, so on.
JIMMY: …I sure missed me that steak n eggs. Over at the steak shack.
YUKI: Aussie style.
JIMMY: They served me all this fuckin' crap at the hospital.
NEVA: Not a four star.
YUKI: Not supposed to be.
JIMMY: Yeah, but they could make an effort. I mean, folks in there are sick n depressed n messed up n lonely, the least they could do is give them some decent food. Somethin' that tastes like somethin'.
ROSALIE: Want a fish tender?
JIMMY: Ain't real.
NEVA: Is too.
JIMMY: I know 'bout fish, Neva. That crumby flaky thing ain't like any fish I ever seen.

YUKI: Pancake batfish.

JIMMY: Mutant kind.

ROSALIE: Jimmy.

JIMMY: What other kind is it?

ROSALIE: I'm eatin.'

JIMMY: I'll taste me a nugget, though.

NEVA: Shouldn't.

JIMMY: Will you quit with that? Ain't my doctor.

YUKI: They treat you good in there, right?

JIMMY: Treat me like anyone else [who] ain't got medical.

ROSALIE: They're overworked, Jimmy.

JIMMY: Ain't no excuse to leave me on some table for an hour, have me waitin' to run a single test.

YUKI: They got their way of doin' things.

JIMMY: You know, Yuki, you shoulda been a lawyer. 'Cuz you sure love defendin' people.

YUKI: Just pointin' out the facts.

JIMMY: I'll see if you tell the same story the day you're in hospital.

NEVA: Don't joke about that.

JIMMY: Just sayin'.

NEVA *(laying down the law)*: Don't.

ROSALIE: …Ray got out of hospital, too.

JIMMY: Yeah?

ROSALIE: Got a call from them up in Waxahachie. Say he's doin' all right, recoverin' a little bit every day.

YUKI: Damn factory fire…

JIMMY: Man, I gotta call him.

ROSALIE: We could visit.

JIMMY: All that way?

ROSALIE: I'll drive. You can just sleep in the car.

JIMMY: We'll see.

ROSALIE: Would be good to visit.

JIMMY: We'll see. … *(refers to flower arrangement)*: Where'd you get those?

ROSALIE: Pretty, right?

JIMMY: Nothin' like real flowers.

ROSALIE: They were at the market. They had a real good assortment of flowers this time. Loved all the bright colors. Not always you can get flowers so bright anymore. Like they glow.

JIMMY: Must've cost quite a bundle.

NEVA: We got 'em, Jimmy.

ROSALIE: I just picked them out.

JIMMY: Don't need hand-out.

YUKI: Not hand-out. Just offerin.'

JIMMY: Win the lottery?

NEVA: Yuki caught some monster fish the other day.

JIMMY: Behind my back?

YUKI: Wadn't monster.

NEVA: Big, right?

YUKI: Bigger than most. That's all.

JIMMY: Sonofabitch.

YUKI: Thought of you, Jimmy.

JIMMY: Half of that catch is mine.

YUKI: What?

JIMMY: We're a team, right?

YUKI: You weren't there, bro.

JIMMY: So, you take it ALL, eh? Rakin' in the dough.

YUKI: One catch. That's all it was. Might not come 'round like that for some time.
JIMMY: But you saw to it I got cut out. Flyin' solo, eh?
YUKI: Not like that.
JIMMY: What's it, then?
YUKI: You were in hospital, man. What you want me to do?
JIMMY: Decent thing.
YUKI: I do the decent thing all the time. I even brought Rosalie here some milk n eggs the other day.
JIMMY: What the hell for?
ROSALIE: Thanks, Yuki.
YUKI: Decent thing. I know how to live my life.
JIMMY: Some kind of saint, eh?
YUKI: Don't push me, man. I got enough shit as it is.
JIMMY: What shit you got? You got your whole life mapped out.
YUKI: What map I got?
JIMMY: Road. You know.
YUKI: Only road I got is Neva and the baby. That's all.
NEVA (with light caress to Yuki): We'll figure it out, honey.
ROSALIE: Still think the flowers are awful nice. Don't you think?
JIMMY: They're all right.
ROSALIE: Coulda never gotten them without...
NEVA: Happy to buy them for you and Jimmy. Special day, after all.
JIMMY: How much you get for?
YUKI: What?

JIMMY: Catch.

YUKI: Still on about that?

JIMMY: How much?

YUKI: Enough for all this and some change.

JIMMY: All this what?

YUKI: All this, man. What you see.

JIMMY: Fried eats, beer and flowers. That's some catch, Yuki.

YUKI: Got lucky, is all.

JIMMY: Should pay you back.

NEVA: It's all right, Jimmy. Don't need.

JIMMY: I wanna. How much all this?

NEVA: Welcome home, bro.

JIMMY: Welcome home, my ass. How much? N the fuckin' milk n eggs you got for Rosalie?

ROSALIE: Take it easy.

JIMMY: I wanna pay you!

NEVA: Don't have to...

JIMMY: *(to Rosalie)* Where's my wallet, honey?

NEVA: Leave that.

JIMMY: Where's my wallet?

ROSALIE: Jimmy.

JIMMY: What?

ROSALIE: We talk about this some other time?

JIMMY: I just wanna pay 'em back, baby.

YUKI: Let sleeping dogs...

JIMMY: Hell with sleeping dogs and their puppies. Wanna do the right thing, Yuki. Can't stand y'all paid for all this and flowers that gonna die anyway too.

YUKI: Catch us on the back end, man.

JIMMY: Back end of what? Christmas? Might not make it 'til then.

ROSALIE: Jimmy.

JIMMY: It's true.

NEVA: Don't know that.

JIMMY: Know what they tell me. I can read their eyes. When them doctors look at me. Now where the hell is my wallet?

ROSALIE: …

JIMMY: What's the mystery, Rosie?

ROSALIE: No mystery.

JIMMY: Then what?

NEVA: Leave be.

JIMMY: WHAT?

YUKI: Don't you yell at her, bro.

JIMMY: Yell how I want, when I want.

ROSALIE: …Five dollars.

JIMMY: What?

ROSALIE: Got five dollars in the house.

JIMMY: What you mean, five dollars? Didn't you sell those flowers that time?

ROSALIE: That money's gone.

JIMMY: Gone where?

ROSALIE: Gone.

JIMMY: You buy some lipstick at the Dollar Store again?

ROSALIE: Bought nothin'.

JIMMY: I go to hospital, and she starts shoppin'.

ROSALIE: Shut the hell up.

JIMMY: What'd you do, baby? Y'all spend all our pocket money?

ROSALIE: Got no idea.

YUKI: Christ. It's just hush puppies and nuggets and… If I can't give you that…

ROSALIE: It's all we got.

JIMMY: Huh?

ROSALIE: …Five dollars.

JIMMY: …All we got we got?

ROSALIE: …

JIMMY: How the hell did that…?

NEVA: She's been tryin', Jimmy.

JIMMY: Sorry?

NEVA: Lotta bills.

JIMMY: Clinic give us a deal.

ROSALIE: I know.

JIMMY: Clinic give us a deal. Said transfer to hospital wouldn't-

ROSALIE: Not on everythin', Jimmy.

JIMMY: I'll talk to them. That's fraudulent business what they done.

ROSALIE: You want I had you taken out of hospital? You had to get tests n treatment and God knows what else, right?

JIMMY: So, it's my fault now?

ROSALIE Didn't say that.

JIMMY: I get sick, I ruin everythin'.

ROSALIE: You're not listenin' to me.

NEVA: She tried, Jimmy.

JIMMY: She tried, she tried… that some song, Neva? How much she try we got five dollars to our name?

ROSALIE: You think I did nothin' while you were in there coughin' up shit? I went me to the swap meet every day. Sold about as much as I could. Stood by the trash, collected cans, even went all the way to the whole other side of the Parish to see if some church would buy some ol' CDs we had....

JIMMY: What you need to do all that for? Got work.

ROSALIE: No work.

JIMMY: Huh?

ROSALIE: Cut my hours. Put me on call.

JIMMY: Why didn't you tell me? Sat there every day in that freeze-ass hospital and you ain't tell me nothin'.

ROSALIE: No use your worryin.'

JIMMY: My worryin'? It's our life, baby. What we gonna do with the house now?

ROSALIE (softly): Ain't.

JIMMY: What?

ROSALIE: Gonna put us out.

A moment.

ROSALIE: I tried to...

JIMMY: Goddamn.

Goddamn sonsofbitches.

Goddamn bank.

Goddamn hospital.

Man can't get sick in this country.

...

Goddamn sonsofbitches did the same to my daddy. He was lyin' on the couch, spittin' up blood, and they were callin' the house "Where's my money? Where's my money?" Like they don't SEE he was dyin', dyin' on that couch, ain't had lick of energy to put one more dime into the cashbox. Goddamn pieces of shit. … This dream, man, this fuckin' dream of water is a lost church. … What the hell we gonna do with five dollars?

Jimmy coughs. Too much.
They wait.
It passes.

ROSALIE: Want some water?
JIMMY: Got beer.
NEVA: Shouldn't.
JIMMY: Drink what I want, Neva! Hell with it. … I'm gonna end up just like my daddy.
ROSALIE: Don't.
JIMMY: All shriveled up on some couch, lookin' at the moon outside his window, dreamin' of some red earth bloomin' somewhere [that] gonna give him peace.
ROSALIE: Don't.
JIMMY: It's the truth, honey. What the hell is wrong with you?
ROSALIE: Not gonna end up like that.
JIMMY: It's cancer. How else I end up?
ROSALIE: They don't know that.
JIMMY: They told me straight to my face. Told us both. You forget that all of a sudden?
ROSALIE: Just think…
JIMMY: Just think, just think… That's what I got.
NEVA: Diagnosis could change.

JIMMY: You a doctor now?
NEVA: Things could stabilize, they could find new drugs...
JIMMY: Cost how much?

He coughs again.

JIMMY (CONT): You're all fuckin' outta your minds.

Followed by a desire to retch, but...
A moment. Nothing.

JIMMY (CONT): Nobody wants a sick man around. Sick man reeks of death. "Stay away, oh angels. Stay away from the destiny of the sick man."
YUKI: What's that?
JIMMY: Somethin' my daddy used to say. He think this whole world gonna sink down under, right down into the bottom of the ocean, like one of those myth fables from long ago. "Long ago on high, the angels cried. Deep unto the well of mystery."
ROSALIE: ...Your daddy never said those things.
JIMMY: Were you there? On his deathbed?

Rosalie rises, walks away.

NEVA: Rosalie?

Rosalie is trying to keep it all in. A moment.
She notices the fake orchid on the ground, off to one side.
She picks it up.

ROSALIE: What's this doin' here? What the fuck is this doin' here?!
JIMMY: What's that?

She starts to tear the orchid apart.

NEVA: Rosalie. Don't.
ROSALIE: Every day. Every goddamn day. Workin n tryin n… Fuckin' shit.

The orchid is destroyed.

JIMMY: Hey.

Jimmy walks over to her slowly.

YUKI: Rosalie?
NEVA: Let them be.

Jimmy begins to pick up the pieces of the flayed orchid.

ROSALIE *(crying)*: What? What you doin'?

He continues, trying to pick up every piece.

JIMMY: You made this.
ROSALIE: Jimmy…

He continues.

ROSALIE (CONT, *gently*): Stop.

JIMMY: You made this.
ROSALIE: Jimmy…

Jimmy finishes picking up the pieces as best he can.
He offers the pieces to Rosalie. Rosalie embraces him.

Scene Seven

Exterior. Day. By the water. The sun is angled in the sky.
The water cracks and ripples. Yuki is fishing. He has
potential hold of a fish, but for some reason it is eluding
him.

YUKI: Come on. Come on. Don't play this game with me. …I'm gonna get you, motherfucker.

Jimmy walks in. He's more deteriorated in his aspect. But
he's determined to fish, anyway: the ritual is necessary.

JIMMY: Gonna wrestle that fish down?
YUKI: What the hell you doin'?
JIMMY: This work, right? This: what I do.
YUKI: You're supposed to be restin'. Doc said…
JIMMY: Doc can say whatever the hell he wants.
Everyone in this town is sick with somethin', all
hackin' n coughin' n spittin' up blood. We ALL gonna
rest? All gonna sleep? Sleep ourselves to hell's what
… What you got? Problem fish?
YUKI: Caught in somethin'.
JIMMY: Ghost net, I bet.

YUKI: Fuckin' dry all mornin'. Not a bite nowhere no-how.
JIMMY: Let me try.
YUKI: If it's caught in a ghost net, gotta pull it, and everythin' with it.
JIMMY: How long I been doin' this, Yuki? I may be sick, but my brain ain't gone yet.

Jimmy tries. A moment. Then…

JIMMY: All tangled to shit down there.
YUKI: What I'd tell you?
JIMMY: Gotta leave it a while. Maybe somethin' come upstream, jostle up against it.
YUKI: …Shit fuckin' day.

Jimmy coughs. Dry hacking cough.

YUKI: Want some…?
JIMMY: Thanks.

Yuki hands him water bottle. Jimmy drinks. He finishes the bottle.

YUKI: Some thirst.
JIMMY: Thirsty all the time now. Won't go away.

A moment. An egret flies over.

JIMMY: Would you look at that?
YUKI: Birds, man.

JIMMY: How do they do it?

YUKI: Do what?

JIMMY: Just keep goin'?

YUKI (*light joke*): Don't pay taxes.

JIMMY: I'm serious.

YUKI: Don't know, man. Don't know.

JIMMY: …Feels good out here.

YUKI: Always got the water.

JIMMY: 'Til it's gone.

YUKI: Aint' gonna be gone.

JIMMY: Gonna be some comic book someday 'bout all this water that used to be here. People are gonna say "Man, that writer is makin' some nasty shit up. That place coulda never existed."

YUKI: …Been here all night, straight to mornin'.

JIMMY: What the hell for?

YUKI: Couldn't sleep. My stomach was all twistin' n turnin'.

JIMMY: Goin' up and down on you?

YUKI: Like someone was stabbin' me in the stomach.

JIMMY: Fuck.

YUKI: I'm, like: I'm gonna head down to the water. I'm up, might as well be up, start the day, y'know? Gotta get some kinda nest egg goin', or we're gonna be flat on our ass when the baby comes.

JIMMY: …Know that.

YUKI: …Didn't mean…

JIMMY: …Ain't got but a day before we're locked out.

YUKI: House? What you doin' here, then?

JIMMY: …

YUKI: What you doin'?

JIMMY: …

YUKI: If you ain't got but a day, you gotta have a plan, Jimmy.

JIMMY: I know.

YUKI: What you gonna do, then?

JIMMY: … Fish.

YUKI: This is serious.

JIMMY: Can't think right now. Can't.

YUKI: …Better start thinkin.'

JIMMY: Fuck you.

YUKI: I'm your friend, man.

JIMMY: Cut me outta that monster fish, though.

YUKI: All right.

Yuki starts gathering his gear and whatever he has at hand, and readies to leave.

JIMMY: Where you-?

YUKI: …No use talkin'.

JIMMY: Hey.

YUKI: No, man. You got your mind made up.

JIMMY: …Didn't mean nothin' by…

YUKI: "Fuck you."

JIMMY: I'm sorry.

YUKI: Not right, bro.

JIMMY: Said I was sorry.

YUKI: All our time here, all these days, years…

JIMMY: Just say things. You know.

YUKI: Say things to say them? … Ain't even supposed to be out here.

JIMMY: Why? Gonna get sick?

Jimmy laughs at his joke, a way to clear the air. The laughter turns into a nasty, dry cough. He laughs.

JIMMY: I'm rotted clear out.
YUKI: Don't mess with that.
JIMMY: It's my mess, I can mess with it anyway I like.
YUKI: Fuckin' punch you, man.
JIMMY: Go on.
YUKI: Make me wanna…
JIMMY: Do it.
YUKI: …don't know what you're sayin.'
JIMMY: I'll take you on.
YUKI: Leave be.
JIMMY: 'Fraid I'll clock you out?
YUKI: Like I gotta be 'fraid of somethin'.
JIMMY: I see you.
YUKI: See me how you like. Not how I am.
JIMMY: What the hell is that? Proverb?
YUKI: No idea.
JIMMY: I'll clock you out. Round and down in the ground.
YUKI: Don't know what [you're]-

Jimmy strikes him. He's weakened physically, but he's daring himself anyway.

YUKI: …All right.
JIMMY: …Just gonna take?
YUKI: Not the time, Jimmy.

Jimmy strikes him again, flailing.

YUKI: ...Not the time.

JIMMY: When the fuck will it be the time? Huh?
When I pull me a Louie Medina and throw myself at
the mercy of the water's tide?

YUKI: Man, you are talkin' some shit.

JIMMY: It's the truth.

YUKI: Louie Medina was swimmin'. Corexit burned
right through him. He didn't throw himself no-where.

JIMMY: ... [I] Got a mind to.

YUKI*(taking it in)*: ...That right?

JIMMY: Got a mind to do a whole lotta things.

YUKI: Got a mind to sit yourself down and wait this
thing out.

JIMMY: Like my daddy? I seen that road, been right
along with it.

A moment.

YUKI: Don't even think about...

JIMMY: Been thinkin.'

YUKI: What about Rosalie? Thinkin' bout her?

JIMMY: Got enough on her hands [to] have to carry
me along, too.

YUKI: Sonofabitch.

JIMMY: What?

YUKI: Sit yourself down, all right? Just sit yourself
down. You're talkin' some kinda nonsense now.

JIMMY: How's what I say-?

YUKI: Can't even be thinkin' bout throwin yourself
into any kinda water, offin' yourself?

JIMMY: Ain't like that.

YUKI: When you got that woman there… That woman loves you, man. Loves you somethin' fierce.
JIMMY: She deserves better. Whole lot better. Deserves nice life. Not this wreck of a thing we got.
YUKI: Ain't a wreck.
JIMMY: You livin' it? … Cast me to the water, man. Let's fuckin' finish me off.
YUKI: Gotta wait this thing out.
JIMMY: Gotta put me on a boat and light the match, like them Vikings way back. Put me out to sea. That's all I want.
YUKI: That what your daddy and your grand-daddy want? They want you to throw yourself into the water? That what they teach you?
JIMMY: My daddy would've done the same, if he could.
YUKI: That may be, but-
JIMMY: It's true. He asked me [to].
The day before he passed,
He said to me "Son, put me out to sea. Let me burn.
Let every part of me tinder itself into the water."
I wouldn't do it.
He begged me.
I still wouldn't do it.
"Selfish boy," he said.
"You're nothin' but a selfish boy."
And he closed his eyes
and didn't speak to me for hours.
I kept lookin' at him, beggin' him to forgive me.
He never did.
YUKI: Won't forgive you now if you…

JIMMY: Huh?

YUKI: Ain't gonna come down from on high and forgive you for doin' to yourself what he wanted done to him.

JIMMY: You up there on high?

YUKI: And if you think it's some kinda protest...

JIMMY: Don't think...

YUKI (CONT): It ain't. And I know, cuz I've been protestin', right? I've been out there, days on end. Ever since Louie Medina passed.

JIMMY: And what it done?

YUKI: Done what it does. It's not for nothing, Jimmy. If you went out there, you'd know. Gives you a kind of strength to spit in their face, call them out.

JIMMY: Yeh?

YUKI: But this, what you're talkin', it's wrong, bro. Plain wrong. A man dyin' is a man dyin'. Whether he dies in a water full of black gold or a bed of feathers in a room full of silver. You wanna lick this thing? You keep on the keep on. All right?

JIMMY: Keep on the keep on 'til I lose my brain altogether, end up some curled-up mess of a thing on some road, twitchin' n shit?

YUKI: Ain't gonna be like that.

JIMMY: That's where I'm headed, man. What you think this mutant cancer thing I got is? I got seven different fuckin' chemicals in my blood, n ALL of them trace themselves back to some form of crude oil or solvent. You hear what I'm sayin'?

YUKI: ... yeh.

JIMMY: So?

YUKI: ...Still think Big Pig can fuck themselves up the ass if they think you or anybody's gonna back down, cast themselves out and into the water for nothin'.
JIMMY: Ain't nothin'.
YUKI: It's nothin', man. Goddamn fuckin' nothin'. How many years you put down here on the water? How many years your daddy and grand-daddy before that? Your whole family, bro. All that's nothin'?
JIMMY: No.
YUKI: Fuck THEM up the fuckin' ass, man. They made us lab rats and we didn't know it. Shame on them. Shame. ... Not on us. Y'hear me?

A moment.

JIMMY: Just think...
YUKI: What?
JIMMY: Where we...?
YUKI: What?
JIMMY: Where we gonna go? ... Once house is ...
YUKI: Stay with us if you need.
JIMMY: No room.
YUKI: Make room.
JIMMY: Can't do that to you, Yuki.
YUKI: How long we go back? Huh? ... You got nowhere to go, I make room for you, y'hear?

Yuki hands Jimmy a handkerchief.

JIMMY: What?

YUKI: You're bleedin'.
JIMMY: Huh?
YUKI: Ear, man.
JIMMY: Thanks.

Jimmy places the handkerchief to his ear, to help stop the blood.

YUKI: You are NOT gonna think about this thing again. All right? ... You listenin'?
JIMMY: Yeh.
YUKI: I am not gonna let you think about it. Fuckin' leave Rosalie alone, leave all of us...

A moment.

YUKI: Finish your time here on this earth, however it come to you, finish it right.
JIMMY: You got no room (in your house).
YUKI: So, go on up to Waxahachie, see your cousin, see what they can do. Just keep on the keep on. Right?

A moment.

JIMMY: Hot.
YUKI: Yeh.
JIMMY: Come tomorrow mornin', we're gonna be out on some road.
YUKI: You'll do fine. You're Jimmy the tiger, right?

Scene Eight

Exterior. Some time before sunrise. In the backyard.
Rosalie has garbage bags in hand. The bags contain all of
her and Jimmy's belongings. She sets the bags down. She's
exhausted. She looks at the yard. The mismatched garden
furniture and cooler are gone. There's nothing left. Nothing
at all. A moment.

ROSALIE *(to herself)*: 'Least it's clean.
JIMMY *(from off, within the house)*: Rosalie?
ROSALIE: What?
JIMMY *(from off, within the house)*: You seen my
headgear?
ROSALIE: Got everythin' here.
JIMMY *(from off, within the house)*: Can't find it.
ROSALIE: Got everythin', Jimmy. You get that little
bag for me by the door, please?
JIMMY *(from off, within the house)*: What's that?
ROSALIE: Little bag. By the door.
She waits. A moment.

ROSALIE: I'll get it.

She goes toward house.

JIMMY *(from off, within the house)*: There's a little bag
here. Want me to bring it out?
ROSALIE: Okay.
JIMMY *(walking in, from house, small drugstore shopper's*
bag in hand): Thought you wanted to leave this.

ROSALIE (takes bag): Those are my things.

Rosalie stuffs little bag into one of the garbage bags.

JIMMY: What things?
ROSALIE: Craft stuff from when I was a little girl.
JIMMY: Why you want that?
ROSALIE: Could sell it.
JIMMY: Nobody buy it.
ROSALIE: Don't know.
JIMMY: They're old, Rosalie.
ROSALIE: Like everythin' else we got.

A moment.

JIMMY: What?
ROSALIE: Tired.
JIMMY: Wanna rest?
ROSALIE: They come round, we gotta be outta here.
Shoulda been outta here already.
JIMMY: We still got time.
ROSALIE: Little bit of time.
JIMMY: If they run us out, they run us out.
ROSALIE: No. I do NOT wanna give them that.
That's what they want. See us runnin', tail between
our legs. No sir. I won't.
JIMMY: Put these in the car, then.
ROSALIE: They're heavy.
JIMMY: I can…

Jimmy lifts one of the garbage bags. It is heavy. He sets it down. He is short of breath.

JIMMY (CONT): What you got in this thing?
ROSALIE: Our stuff.
JIMMY: What kinda stuff?
ROSALIE: Towels and hardware and spoons and cups and... you know.
JIMMY: Throw this out.
ROSALIE: What?
JIMMY: What we gonna do with all this?
ROSALIE: Use it.
JIMMY: Don't fit in the car.
ROSALIE: I'll get it.

She lifts the garbage bag. It is heavy, unwieldy. She struggles, but manages regardless.

JIMMY: Will you stop that? ... Rosalie?
ROSALIE: I'll put it in the trunk. I'll make it fit.
   Rosalie walks towards car, unseen, with garbage bag in hand. Jimmy looks at her.

JIMMY: Penguin.
ROSALIE: Huh?
JIMMY: Walkin' like a... penguin.
ROSALIE *(playful)*: Shut up.

She is now out of view. Jimmy looks about the yard. Drops of rain fall from the sky. Is it real rain, or does only Jimmy feel it?

JIMMY *(feeling rain, startled by it)*: What the hell?
ROSALIE *(from Off)*: You call me?
JIMMY: Rainin.'
ROSALIE *(from off)*: Gonna fit just fine.
JIMMY *(refers to the rain)*: Stings.
ROSALIE *(from Off)*: I always said this car got more give than we give it credit.

He's dizzy for a moment. Loses his bearings. Falls.

JIMMY: Sonofabitch.

He laughs. Rosalie walks in. Sees him on the ground, laughing.

ROSALIE: Jimmy?
JIMMY: Sonofabitch.

He's still laughing.

ROSALIE: What's goin' on, eh? What happened?
JIMMY: ...Rainin.'
ROSALIE: Not rainin.' It's dry 'n humid as all get. Not a speck of rain out here.
JIMMY: Later.
ROSALIE: Huh?
JIMMY: Gonna rain later.
ROSALIE: You're the forecaster now?
JIMMY: Get me a job.
ROSALIE: Fisherman to forecaster. Watch out world.
JIMMY: Hey.

ROSALIE: I'm gonna put the other bag in the car.
JIMMY: Hey.
ROSALIE: What?
JIMMY: Stay.
ROSALIE: Jimmy, I gotta…
JIMMY: We got time.
ROSALIE: This ain't no game, Jimmy. They're gonna lock the door and shut us out.
JIMMY: Early. Sun's not even up yet.
ROSALIE: Gonna be.
JIMMY: Sit.
ROSALIE: Jimmy.
JIMMY: Come on.
ROSALIE: You want us to sit in the yard like a pair of kids?
JIMMY: We used to in high school.
ROSALIE: Just kids, then.
JIMMY: So?
ROSALIE: … Well. Just a little while. But then, we gotta get goin', cuz I will NOT give them the satisfaction-
JIMMY: I know. … I know.

A moment.

JIMMY (CONT): Feels nice, right?
ROSALIE: It's our yard.
JIMMY: So quiet.
ROSALIE: Everybody's sleepin'.
JIMMY: Peaceful.
ROSALIE: Like church.

JIMMY: Not like church.

ROSALIE: Sometimes. Like, when you go in and there's no one there… just you and prayer fillin' up the space.

Rosalie caresses his hair.

ROSALIE: You comb this thing?
JIMMY: Huh?
ROSALIE It's all tangled.
JIMMY: Run your fingers through.
ROSALIE: Gonna look like I run my fingers through.
JIMMY: That's all right.

Rosalie combs through his hair with her fingers.

ROSALIE *(refers to his hair)*: Thinnin.'
JIMMY: Gettin' old.
ROSALIE: Don't know anybody who gets young.

She absently hums a little song as she does so.

JIMMY: What's that?
ROSALIE: …?
JIMMY: Song.
ROSALIE: Don't know.
JIMMY: Sounded nice.
ROSALIE: So many songs stuck in my head.
JIMMY: We could recite them all.
ROSALIE *(finishing the comb through)*: Fill up a book.
JIMMY: Remember when we used to do that?

ROSALIE: …?
JIMMY: Back when we first startin' hookin' up.
Recitin' songs.
ROSALIE: Did we do that?
JIMMY: *nods.*
ROSALIE: You sure that wasn't with Neva?
JIMMY: Hell no.
ROSALIE: Crazy thing to do.
JIMMY: You don't remember? We'd try to recite them
all, all the titles, the minute they came into our head.
Rule was we couldn't stop. Just let them keep flowin',
as we shouted them up to the sky.
ROSALIE: This must've been with some other girl.
JIMMY: No. It wadn't.
We'd lay on the ground,
Out over by the edge of the football field,
Back where the goldenrods were in bloom,
And we'd shout all these songs into the air,
Testin' ourselves, testin' everythin' around us,
And the cicadas would join in, makin' their sound,
Creatin' some kinda weird symphony,
'Til we'd hear someone say "Quit that racket."
And then we'd laugh n nestle into each other,
Your perfume hittin' my nose just right,
N we'd close our eyes, n pretend to sleep,
N pretend the sky was some kind of brilliant archive
ROSALIE: Archive?
JIMMY: Like a big library or somethin'.
ROSALIE: I can see it.
JIMMY: N this library could hang onto all our songs
N send them down at whatever time we needed;

ROSALIE: Nice library.

JIMMY: N you'd run your fingers across my chest
And whisper all these dreams you had in your head,
Stuff I had no idea about,
Stuff that blew my mind.
Stuff 'bout travelin' to places n designin'… *(finding the word in memory)* atriums,

ROSALIE: Huh?

JIMMY: Full of butterfly peas n cattails n sea oats n rabbits-

ROSALIE: I must've been drunk.

JIMMY: N then we'd pretend the songs would rain down on us
From the sky n cover us with their music
N make us feel special,
Like, everythin' we did, had done, or dreamt of,
Really mattered, really fuckin' mattered in the world,
N I'd say "I'm gonna build you a house
That looks onto the water,
so you can see me fish every day,
N there won't be anythin' you'll ever need for."

A moment.

ROSALIE: That was a long time ago.

JIMMY: You remember, then?

ROSALIE: I remember you held me, like: gloomy
Monday mornin' I'm in love with a boy who loves the
sun n don't think twice, it's all right, cuz the sun's in
my eyes and he ain't gonna leave me high n dry.
Shared, simple laughter.

A moment.
Intimacy or tenderness between them.
He starts shaking.
She holds him.
After brief moment, the shaking subsides.
And then…

ROSALIE: We gotta get goin'.
JIMMY: …I'll stay here.
ROSALIE: What?
JIMMY: Go on.
ROSALIE: Jimmy. What are you talkin' about?
JIMMY: Won't make it.
ROSALIE: You'll make it. If I have to carry you all the way, you're gonna make it.
JIMMY: Carry me in the car?
ROSALIE: Come on.
JIMMY: My leg's asleep.
ROSALIE: So? Wake it up.
JIMMY *(temporary paralysis)*: Can't move it.
ROSALIE: Try to stretch.
JIMMY: Won't.
ROSALIE: Give here.
JIMMY: Huh?
ROSALIE: Come on.

Rosalie helps him up.

ROSALIE: How's that?
JIMMY: Freaky.
ROSALIE: Earth movin' around?

JIMMY: Movin' in bits ...
ROSALIE: It's all right.
JIMMY: How can you-?
ROSALIE: It'll steady itself out. In time. You'll see.

Rosalie grabs remaining garbage bag.

JIMMY: Let me.
ROSALIE: I got it.
JIMMY: Wanna help.
ROSALIE: You know how you help me?
JIMMY: ...?
ROSALIE *(playful)*: By not helpin'.
JIMMY *(playful in kind)*: Fulla shit.
ROSALIE: Come on.
JIMMY: ... Does it have to be Waxahachie?
ROSALIE: That's where your cousin is. They got room.
JIMMY: What if the car gives out on the way?
ROSALIE: Won't.
JIMMY: Motor's a piece of shit.
ROSALIE: Then we'll end up where we end up.
         They start to walk away. Jimmy stops.
JIMMY (CONT): What's that?
ROSALIE: Huh?
JIMMY: In the sky
ROSALIE: Don't see nothin'.
JIMMY: Right there. ... See?

As sun is about to rise,
a green ray of light is seen, across the sky

For a few seconds, and then, it's gone.

ROSALIE *(almost to herself)*: Green ray. Pretty.
JIMMY: Made a wish?
ROSALIE: Huh?
JIMMY: Like your auntie taught you?
ROSALIE: Maybe.
JIMMY: Gotta wish things.
ROSALIE: If you say.
JIMMY: All we got, right?
ROSALIE: … We gotta go.
JIMMY: … … Made a sign.
ROSALIE: …?
JIMMY: For the protest.
ROSALIE: What?
JIMMY: Wanted to make something.
ROSALIE: Where's it at?
JIMMY: Back seat.
ROSALIE: Where back seat?
JIMMY: Tucked under.
ROSALIE *(playful)*: Hidin' things from me, mister man?
JIMMY *(in kind: a glimmer of former self)*: All sorts of things, *(sings an improvised tune)* Rosalie, Rosalie, sweet as a honey bee…
ROSALIE: … Protest, eh? Wanna stop on over there before we head out?
JIMMY: Yeah.

Lights fade.

CPSIA information can be obtained
at www.ICGtesting.com
Printed in the USA
LVOW12s1717290617
539815LV00002B/315/P